THE C
FRO
THE PO

By
R.H. Lawson

Artwork by RHL

CONTENTS

About the Author

About the Legendary R.H. Lawson.

Hailed as the greatest fantasy writer of the past thousand years, R.H. Lawson is the universally celebrated author behind the genre-defining masterpiece, "The Call from the Portal."

Born to a family of mystical druids on a particularly stormy night under a crimson moon, R.H. displayed powerful magical abilities from an early age. After accidentally turning his childhood nemesis into a newt at the age of 7, he was sent away to be trained in spell casting and potion brewing at an elite secret academy, hidden deep within an enchanted forest.
After graduating top of his class in wizardry, R.H. set off globetrotting to research mythology and folklore.

R.H. spent his later years adventuring across a multitude of mythical realms where he won the legendary Totem of Destiny in an epic rap battle against the Norse God Odin.
When not dictating his manuscripts to a quill-wielding marmoset familiar, R.H. enjoys BASE jumping off floating mountains, and competing in illegal underground unicorn races. (No mythical beasts are harmed during such events, in fact Unicorns are surprisingly competitive!)

Now settled in a haunted Scottish castle surrounded by a petting zoo of fantastical beasts, R.H. is hard at work on his upcoming fantasy saga, projected to be the best-selling book series of the next two millennia.

When asked about the inspiration for his writing, R.H. says:
"I channel the prose directly from my mind's eye, after imbibing a bubbling cocktail of dragon tears and pixie dust.
The words just flow through me and onto the page. My fingers are but a conduit for the Muse's genius or dare I say, the divine inspiration.

And to you my beloved reader, I wish you the greatest of fortunes until we meet again, in the next adventure."

Love,
RHL

Feel free to visit the authors page https://www.amazon.com/author/richardhoughtonlawson where you can use the 'Follow' button to discover what's new and hot from the amazing imagination of the greatest and most humble fantasy scribe the world has ever known!

CHAPTER 1

Flickering Lights

Amelia stared anxiously out of the car window as her dad pulled into the driveway of yet another new house, in yet another new town.
She'd lost count of how many times they had uprooted their lives because of her dad's job.
Just when she would start to settle in, make a few friends, and feel comfortable at school, it was time to say goodbye again.

Fortunately, in this town she at least had one friend, Julia, whose dad Henry had moved their family here the year previously.
Julia and Amelia had kept in touch texting back and forth and they'd also managed a fun day out at the huge shopping centre that lay roughly between their homes on either side of town, both of them needing to catch a long boring bus ride to spend the day together.

"I know this isn't easy, honey," her dad said, putting the car in park and turning around to face her. "But I promise this is the last move. I was able to negotiate a permanent transfer with my company."

Amelia forced a smile and nodded. She wanted to believe him but had heard those promises before. Still, maybe this time would be different.
Either way, she took a deep breath, slung her backpack over her shoulder, and headed towards the looming new brick building that would be her high school.
Time to start the exhausting process of adapting all over again.

The harsh fluorescent lights of the hallways burned Amelia's eyes, a stark contrast to the cozy darkness of the car ride over.
Students laughed and chatted loudly with their friends, oblivious to the new girl nervously trying to find her assigned locker.
Amelia felt invisible, just another nameless stranger intruding on their established social landscape.
Trying to calm her own nerves, Amelia's mind drifted fondly to her friend Julia.

She remembered when they were much younger, giggling wildly while building hidden blanket forts in her bedroom.
Julia was always the braver one, leading them on backyard adventures hunting for fairies and climbing trees together.
Amelia smiled, recalling late night sleepovers where she and Julia would stay up way past their bedtimes whispering secrets and fears only a best friend would understand.
Julia helped Amelia believe in herself when her confidence faltered.

The shrill sound of the bell jolted Amelia back to the present.
She took a deep steadying breath, picturing Julia's playful smile and infectious optimism.

By the time she'd slid into her seat in first period English class, Amelia's stomach was churning.
She kept her eyes down, avoiding making contact with the other students taking their seats around her.
Amelia dreaded the inevitable moment when the teacher would introduce her and make her recite some "fun facts" about herself to the class. It was a familiar routine by now, but no less painful.

Right on cue, Mrs. Evans smiled kindly and said "Class, I'd like you all to welcome a new student joining us at Forest View High.
Amelia, would you like to stand up and tell us a little bit about yourself?"

Amelia's heart pounded as she reluctantly stood up, acutely aware of all the eyes now turned in her direction.
"Um, hi. I'm Amelia. My family just moved here..." She stumbled through mentioning a couple of hobbies and where she had lived before, cringing internally at revealing how many different towns she had shuffled through over the years.
A few students giggled quietly, which only helped to increase her embarrassment.

Mercifully, the bell rang signalling the end of class before Amelia had to answer any questions.
She quickly gathered her things, exhaling with relief now that the awful introduction was over.
She just had to get through the rest of this first day, she told herself.

Starting over at a new school never got easier, but at least the day was already partway done.

During lunch period, Amelia grabbed some food and found an empty table at the edge of the crowded cafeteria.
As she picked half-heartedly at her meal, she overheard a group of popular girls whispering nearby and glancing her way.

"She seems kind of weird, always moving around like that," one girl remarked snarkily, just loud enough for Amelia to hear.
"My brother said she was homeschooled for a couple years too. Total weirdo loner type."

Amelia felt her cheeks burn with embarrassment and anger.
No matter how hard she tried to just keep her head down, it was never enough.
She was forever destined to be the outcast, the perpetual new girl judged for circumstances beyond her control.
All she wanted was to find a real home for once, a place where she could be accepted as more than just the introverted drifter kid.
But maybe fitting in just wasn't her fate.

At long last, the final bell rang, releasing Amelia from the social purgatory of her first day.
As she waited by the curb for her mum's minivan to pull up, she noticed some flickering lights coming from within the woodland behind the schools' buildings.
Squinting into the trees, she was reminded of a traveling fairground and wondered if one might be visiting this new town.

Before she could investigate further, her mum arrived, greeting Amelia with her usual cheeriness. "How was your first day? Make any new friends yet?" she asked brightly, clearly trying to keep Amelia's spirits up.
"Oh, you know, it was fine," Amelia lied, forcing a smile as she got into the passenger seat.

Once home, Amelia retreated to the solace of her bedroom. She eagerly picked up her beloved guitar, running her fingers gently over the smooth wooden neck.

Strumming a few chords, she began singing softly, allowing the music to transport her.
When it was just Amelia alone with her guitar, she felt free to belt out lyrics with abandon.
Music was her refuge, a means of expressing emotions too complex for words.
She sang for hours, only stopping once her voice grew hoarse and fingers sore.

That night in bed she drifted off into a fitful bout of sleep, dreaming about fairground lights like the ones she'd spotted in the woodlands near her new school.

The following morning Amelia's eyes snapped open to the blaring of her alarm.
She fumbled on the nightstand to hit snooze and buy herself a few more minutes of precious sleep. But soon her mum's voice echoed up the stairs.

"Amelia! Time to get up or you'll miss the bus!"

With a groan, Amelia dragged herself out of bed.
She caught a glimpse of her reflection in the mirror and cringed at the rat's nest of dark hair framing her exhausted face.
Why did high school have to start so early? Was it some form of cruel and unusual punishment?

After half-heartedly trying to smooth down her hair, Amelia splashed some water on her face and threw on a hoodie and jeans.
She could already tell it was going to be one of those days where she felt completely disconnected from everything around her.

Trudging into the kitchen, Amelia found her younger brother Cole at the table engrossed in something on his phone as usual.
He was always absorbed in social media and random gaming videos.
Though they bickered at times, Cole and Amelia shared a close bond.
As kids, they were constant playmates, making up elaborate games of make-believe.
They'd team up for epic snowball fights in winter and defended each other from bullies at school.

Whenever they could get away with it, they would stay up late sharing secrets.

Now a little older, their relationship had evolved.
Cole was popular and outgoing, while Amelia was introverted.
But she admired his ability to make friends easily. And Cole appreciated his sister's creative spirit and loyalty.

"Look who's finally awake," he said, not even glancing up from his device.
"Have a nice long hibernation?"

Amelia rolled her eyes dramatically. Underneath the teasing tone, there was affection.
"Not long enough," she muttered as she grabbed a yogurt from the fridge.

Cole chuckled, casting her a quick smile.
Though different in temperament, their sibling bond ran deep.
They balanced each other out and always had the other's back when it mattered most.

Amelia's dad peered at her over his newspaper with a bemused expression.
"You're wearing that? on only your second day of a new school," he said, raising an eyebrow.

Amelia shrugged and flopped down in the chair across from Cole.
"It's just school, Dad. No one cares what I wear."

She picked at her yogurt, too tired to have much of an appetite.
The thought of walking those new dreary high school halls and trying not to fall asleep in the first period history class already had her drained.
The only silver lining would be getting to meet up with her friend Julia after school and tell her all about the fairground she might have found.

Her phone buzzed.
It was Julia, frantically triple-texting about a hot new student that had just joined her school. Apparently, he too had just moved into town with his family.
Amelia had to admit it piqued her curiosity but he was at Julia's school across town and not hers, she sighed a little.

"Make good choices today!" her dad called out as Amelia slung her backpack over her shoulder and headed to the bus stop at the end of the street.
She gave a half-hearted wave without looking back.

As the school bus pulled up, she took a deep breath, put her headphones on and cranked up her favourite playlist to drown out the world around her.
She stared out of the window watching the trees go by, steeling herself for another tedious day of classes.

Amelia floated through the first part of her day in a total haze, barely staying awake through some of the lessons.
In history, Mr. Fletcher droned on about Revolutionary war battles, whilst Amelia doodled idly in her notebook, sketching a fantastical creature with the wings of a dragon, head of an eagle and body of a horse.
Colouring it in with her favourite sparkly gel pens soothed her restlessness.
Amelia loved collecting unique notebooks and stationery.
Doodling helped her zone out, filling page after page with whimsical creatures, floral patterns and mandalas.
She could get lost for hours embellishing her notebooks with glitter and stickers.
She found that bringing these inanimate objects to life through art was immensely satisfying.

Amelia glanced periodically out of the classroom window and also at the large clock on the classroom wall.
Still ten more minutes left in this mind-numbing history class, she thought.
There they were again! The flickering lights shining through the trees by the edge of campus.
Maybe she could get Julia to explore them with her after school.
Amelia raised her hand and made her excuses to use the toilet, once there she quickly messaged Julia to meet her after school by the big oak tree in the courtyard of her new school.

When at last the final bell rang, Amelia shoved her books into her locker and made her way to the large oak tree to wait.
After what seemed like an eternity and several messages back and forth discussing bus times, her bubbly blonde friend came bounding up to her.

“Oh my gosh, you have to see this new guy Callum” Julia gushed, her blue eyes lighting up as she opened a picture on her phone.
“Isn’t he just as cute as I said. And that luscious black hair!”
Amelia smiled indulgently.

Only last month, Julia had messaged Amelia about how she been given detention for sneaking away from a field trip to meet a boy she'd been messaging online.
Julia's optimistic enthusiasm sometimes led her to plunge headfirst into situations without thinking them through.
Her impulsiveness sometimes got her into trouble, but she always bounced back, cheerful as ever.

“Hey Julia, I’ve noticed some flickering lights coming from the woodlands by school. They looked kind of bizarre, maybe a travelling fairground?
Want to come and check them out with me?”

Julia’s eyes widened. “Ooh, mysterious! Could be something cool out there. Let’s do it!” She was always up for adventures.

The two girls made their way across the campus, the trees looming closer. As they reached the edge of the woodland, the flickering lights seemed to glow a little brighter just up ahead.

Exchanging mildly apprehensive glances, Amelia and Julia ventured into the trees, the leaves and twigs crunching under the weight of their feet as they stepped in.

CHAPTER 2

Crossing Over

As they went deeper, the sunlight became sparse, filtering through the leafy canopy and giving the woods an eerie, otherworldly aura.

"This is...really creepy," Julia whispered as they pressed on further into the gloom.
But the curiosity was too powerful to turn back now.

The flickering light led them further into the unfamiliar woodland until they arrived at a small clearing.
There in the centre stood a solitary tree, ancient and gnarled, its bark weathered by centuries of storms.
Knotholes yawned in the trunk like gaping mouths, from which rays of shimmering light leaked into the moist forest air, dust glittering in them like tiny fireflies.

Amelia and Julia now clasping one another tightly stepped a little closer and as they did, the tree seemed to hum with an arcane energy, vibrating with the resonance of a plucked harp string.
The girls began to slowly circle around it, eyeing it with growing suspicion.
Upon reaching the far side they stopped, realising that the trunk was hollow with an opening that gazed at them like a giant unblinking eye.
The girls glanced at each other then back at the opening.
Julia could no longer resist and stooped forward, still holding Amelias hand tightly, she peered in.

"What the heck is it?!" Amelia asked her heart pounding.
Julia mumbled something incomprehensible as her brain struggled to catch up with what she was seeing, right there inside the hollow tree was a pulsating orb of pure energy that seemed to inhale and exhale with a soundless rhythm, beckoning her toward it.
Julia held her breath as she reached her hand in.

Suddenly a blinding white flash enveloped them as if hundreds of cameras had all fired at once.
When the spots cleared from their vision, the girls saw they were standing in an incredible meadow filled with luminescent lilac grass and unfamiliar flowers under an alien looking sky.
There was no sign of the woodland nor the ancient gnarled tree.

"I really don't think we're in Kansas anymore," Amelia muttered in awe.
She had no idea where this mystical place was, how they got here, or how to get back home.
But one thing was certain, this was no longer their hometown.

Julia turned in a slow circle, mouth agape.
"Any ideas where we are?" she asked faintly. "This is like something out of a fantasy novel. Are we even on Earth?"

Amelia shook her head, at a total loss.
"I've... I've no idea she stuttered but isn't that someone coming towards us?" Her voice trailing off nervously.

Julia shaded her eyes with her hand and squinted into the distance, then she too noticed a shining figure approaching them through the meadow.
The woman glowed with an unearthly radiance, dressed in ethereal robes.

"Greetings. I am Faven, a light spirit," the woman introduced herself in a melodic voice.
"You have crossed over into the magical Realm of Reflections. Come, you have much to learn."

Exchanging stunned looks, Amelia and Julia cautiously followed Faven, towards what appeared in the distance to be some sort of shimmering crystal-like buildings.
Amelia's mind raced with questions.
How long would they be trapped here?
What awaited them in this bizarre place?
Would they ever find their way back home?

Faven led Amelia and Julia through the alien meadow towards a magnificent crystal structure that glimmered in the near distance.

As they walked, the grass shifted colours around them, cycling through vibrant hues of violet, azure, and emerald.

As they continued walking, Faven began explaining the nature of the magical realm with Amelia and Julia.

"This is the Realm of Reflections, a plane that exists parallel to your own world but it is infused with elemental magic," she said in her gentle, melodic voice.

"Here, magic is a living energy that connects all beings and places. Some individuals have an innate gift to manipulate these magical forces and there are artifacts here that can store magic to be harnessed when needed.
The crystal city we approach amplifies magic, as it is built upon a nexus of powerful arcane energies."

Faven went on to describe how magic could be used for good or ill depending on the mindset of the wielder.
"When handled responsibly, magic brings healing, creation and light. But in corrupted hands, it becomes a tool for harm, destruction and darkness."

She explained that malevolent beings could taint magic by channelling negative emotions like fear, hate and anger.
"This twisting of magic's intended purpose disrupts the harmony of our realm. But magic that comes from positivity, like love, courage and hope, flows in alignment with the natural order of our realm."

As they drew nearer to the glimmering crystal city, Amelia and Julia listened in rapt attention, trying to absorb everything about the workings of magic in this fascinating new place.

“How...why are we here?” Amelia stammered, struggling to comprehend everything.
Her mind was still reeling.

Faven smiled kindly.
“The portal you discovered acts as a gateway between realms. Not all humans can see the light of the portals beacon, you were drawn here for a purpose, one that will soon be revealed to you.”

Julia kept nervously fiddling with her hair, her usual chatter silenced by the shock of their unbelievable situation.
Amelia reached over and gave her hand a reassuring squeeze.

Soon, they'd arrived at their gleaming destination.

As they continued to follow Faven, passing through beautiful archways and corridors that seemed alive with flickering light, other ethereal figures glided silently through the halls, nodding in greeting.
The interior was stunning, with rainbow-hued windows and intriguing glowing symbols adorning the walls.
Amelia felt totally disoriented.
Just this morning she'd been eating breakfast at home, and now here she was in some magical city in another world!

"Come, you must meet the Guardians."
Faven ushered them toward an opulent chamber draped in shimmering fabrics.
Waiting inside were three more angelic figures who immediately turned their piercing gazes upon the girls.
"Welcome Amelia and Julia," said the tallest Guardian in a booming yet gentle voice.
"We are the realm Guardians. I am Balan, joined by my brothers Torin and Valdis."
The other two inclined their heads graciously.

Amelia nervously met their eyes.
"Can you please explain why we're here and how we can get home as soon as possible?"
Julia nodded vigorously in agreement.

The three Guardians exchanged solemn looks.
Torin stepped forward, his emerald robes swirling around him.
"You two possess a unique energy within your auras, an energy this realm needs in order to restore balance and harmony."

Seeing their confused expressions, Valdis elaborated.

"Our world maintains equilibrium through positive energy from physical visitors. Of late our realm has begun being overrun by...dark forces. Your presence here can help readdress the balance."

Amelia's mind raced to absorb all of this.
Her? Julia? Restore magical balance to this parallel world?
Surely they had the wrong ordinary teenagers!

As if reading her uncertainty, Balan smiled kindly.
"Have faith in your abilities. We shall help guide you on your journey to bring light and magical balance back to our realm."

Julia finally found her voice again.
"But what about getting home? Our families will be worried sick!"

Torin waved his hand and a vision swirled before them; it was the portal site back on Earth.

"Time moves differently between the realms," he explained.
"Once you complete this task, the portal will reopen to the same exact moment of your leaving, and you will be reunited with your world."
"It is not our intention for you to be trapped here but until sufficient magical balance has been restored across the realm, the portal simply does not have the energy available to return you both at this time."

Amelia felt a nervous flutter in her stomach. This was a lot to take in.
She met Julia's eyes and a silent understanding passed between them.
Whatever this bizarre quest entailed, she felt that together they would have to tackle it to have any hope of getting back home again.
Surely her and Julia could, she thought, they'd managed to overcome problems before when they both put their minds to it.

"Erm...okay, so tell us, what is it we're supposed to do here," Amelia said, lifting herself up straighter and raising her chin as determinedly as she felt she could muster at this moment in time.
Although her knees didn't feel entirely stable at this very moment, she wasn't going to let this realm suffer needlessly if she could help it, no matter how bizarre and unnerving this entire situation seemed.
It beat suffering yet another day at her new school anyway, she thought.

“Yes” she reassured herself, me and Julia, we can do this and then get back home safe and sound, no one would know the difference, and no one would believe us anyway, she broke into an unsure laugh at the craziness of it all.

The Guardians' faces shone with a mixture of renewed hope and relief.
“You possess courageous hearts,” Valdis praised.
“We will help prepare you. But first, allow us to have you shown to your new quarters where you can get settled in and process all that you have learned.”

Still somewhat bemused, Amelia and Julia followed another light spirit who ushered them down crystalline halls to a beautiful room with two beds that seemed to be moulded from pure crystal.
Exhausted emotionally and physically from the intensity of the day's events, they both collapsed onto the soft, cloud-like mattresses.
Within moments, Julia was face down in her pillow, asleep.

But Amelia's mind kept racing. Would she really rise to this task and help play her part in saving a strange magical world?
Was any of this even real?
The weight of the Guardians' faith in her pressed down, filling her with a strange mixture of pride and uncertainty.
As she finally drifted off, Amelia hoped that when morning came, she’d awaken in her cosy bed back at home.
But deep down, she feared this was real and only just beginning.

CHAPTER 3

The Realm of Reflections

Brilliant morning light filtered into the crystalline bedchamber, stirring Amelia from sleep.

For a brief moment she forgot where she was. But seeing Julia in the bed next to hers quickly jolted her memory back. They were still in this surreal Realm of Reflections!

As the girls got ready, Faven arrived to escort them to breakfast.
Her melodic voice rang out cheerfully, "Good morning my young friends! I trust you both rested well after yesterday's momentous events?"

Amelia and Julia exchanged glances, still feeling disoriented.

"We slept alright," Amelia said hesitantly.
"Still feels a bit strange being in this magical place."

"Quite understandable," Faven replied with an empathetic smile.
"I'm sure it must be quite overwhelming.
But in time, you'll adjust and this realm will start to feel like a second home."

"I hope so," said Julia, sounding uncertain.
"Everything here is just so...so unbelievable!"

Faven squeezed both their hands warmly.
"I know this is a tremendous amount to take in. But I have faith you two will rise to meet the challenges ahead.
Now come, let us breakfast together and continue discussing your purpose here."

They followed Faven through the glittering halls, taking in the splendour around them.
“This place is unbelievable,” Julia murmured, trailing her hand along a shimmering wall.

"Like a fairy tale world."
Upon reaching the dining chamber, they were greeted by a large spread of strange looking fruits, each with differing jewel-toned skins, the first bite revealed them to be deliciously sweet and juicy. As they ate, the three Guardians arrived.

"I trust you're now well rested?" said Balan.
Amelia and Julia nodded hesitantly.
"Splendid! He replied, "Then let us further explain your purpose here."

Torin conjured a glowing image of a dark, fiery pit.
"This is the Maelstrom, a void that has been slowly corrupting our realm, feeding off chaotic energy and negative thoughts."
"Your presence here disrupts the Maelstrom's power," Valdis continued. "Those sweet fruits you're eating are special to your kind and will help to amplify your energy from positive thoughts and deeds, so conduct yourselves with good intent and care whilst you're here."
"You must travel to sacred sites throughout the realm to spread your unique positive light energies. This is the only way to suppress and readdress the dark forces that have begun taking root."

Amelia's stomach dropped even as she felt a sense of duty settle over her.
"Dark forces" ... Julia said, her expression changing as if the delicious fruits had become sour.

"Where must we go to first," Amelia asked, slowly meeting the Guardians' eyes with a wavering expression of confidence, belying her inner feelings of disbelief in what they were even agreeing to.

Balan waved his hand like the conductor of an orchestra and a detailed map appeared, floating in the air before them.
"You must start in the Verdant Forest and revive the Crystal Shrine, then make your way to the Mirror Lakes to awaken the Twilight Sanctum, Faven will accompany you to act as your guide."

As he further outlined their journey, Amelia felt overwhelmed but surprising even to herself, quite resolute.
She was still sceptical that any of this was real, yet some part of her wanted to embrace this new call to adventure.

Before long Faven arrived, followed by a floating sled of various colourful parcels, she smiled and explained they would need these provisions for their travels.
“Erm, travels?” said Julia starting to nibble at her bottom lip, “Just how far away is this place we’re going to?”
“We’ll be there soon enough,” replied Faven and without any further explanation she was leading the girls out of the palatial city and onward towards their first destination.

As they journeyed through meadows and pleasant rolling valleys, the scenery shifted from a plush paradise to increasingly ominous dead woods.

“The Maelstrom’s influence corrupts everything it touches, and we need to get to the bottom of its source” Faven sighed sadly, her hand caressing a dying tree as she passed.
They pressed on until the decaying forest began thinning out, finally opening up into a breathtaking glade. Lush grass and flowers swayed as if still blessed with magic’s touch.

At its centre stood an ancient shrine, its once smooth stone surface now cracked and eroded by the passage of countless seasons.
Intricate runes and symbols etched into the weathered rock were barely visible anymore, obscured by creeping vines that clung to the shrine like a web.

Clustered beneath this organic lattice work of thorny vines, Amelia could glimpse a matrix of cloudy crystals, their inner fire dim and dormant, reduced to ruin by the dark wearisome effect of the Maelstrom.

This must be the Crystal Shrine, thought Amelia.
She hesitated for a moment, daunted by the decrepit state of the hallowed relic.
Then she steeled herself, knowing the shrine's restoration depended on her commitment.

Gingerly, she pried away the tenacious vines, wincing as thorns sliced her fingers.

She could sense the crystals' faint vibrations through the tips of her fingers as she edged them closer to the shrines surface.

Laying her bloodied palms upon the cracked central stone and its matrix of clouded crystals, Amelia emptied her mind and focused her spirit with thoughts of loving kindness.
Warmth blossomed inside her core and radiated outward. The vines visibly recoiled from her touch and the crystals began to hum.

Hope soared within her, but just as quickly turned to ash.
The shrine's runes flickered briefly then dimmed again.
Her brief surge of magical energy had vanished like mist.

Dismayed, Amelia slumped to her knees, her fingers stinging.
The neglected shrine's restoration would require more than a flicker of energy.
She had failed her first real test.

Sensing her friend's despair, Julia squeezed Amelia's shoulder reassuringly. "Hey, don't lose faith. Just slow down, take your time."

With Julia's encouraging words, Amelia shut her eyes, tuning out her doubts. She inhaled deeply then exhaled fully, matching her breath to the shrine's languid, ageless pulse.
She tuned in again to the subtle tingles she could feel emanating from the crystals vibrations.

Gradually she understood, brute force would not reignite this lost light.
She had to coax it gently like a flickering candle flame.
When Amelia opened her eyes once more, serene resolve flowed through her as her palms pressed tenderly on the shrines surface, she let her energy seep slowly into the ancient stone.

A high-pitched melody rang out as the shrine began awakening until brilliant light blazed forth from the rapidly rejuvenating crystals, banishing the gloom from the glade.

“Wow,” Julia gasped.
“Your true energy Amelia,” added Faven joyously.

Amelia blinked in astonishment as the distant woods sprang back to life and even the glade around her seemed to glow with greater vitality, as a pulse of light energy travelled outwardly through the ground in an expanding circular wave.
She had in fact passed her first test, Amelia thought, smiling modestly yet feeling stronger in herself, as her eyes met Julia and Favens.

Dusk began to slowly edge in as Faven guided the group to a suitable spot to make camp for the night.
Faven waved her hands and several of the packages drifted from the sled then began unpacking themselves becoming tall slender tents of the finest translucent silks, each containing a plump looking bed, small table and ornate storage chest.
Faven then closed her eyes and made some unusual gestures with her hands, which conjured into the air around the tents, a string of colourful glowing light orbs, which cast soft hues into the camp.

Faven smiled as she viewed Amelia and Julia's expressions at what had just unfolded before their very eyes.
"Would you like to learn how to create light orbs?" Faven asked in her usual soothing tone.
"Yeh!" the girls agreed in unison.
Faven carefully showed them the hand patterns to make, repeating the movements several times until Amelia and Julia both had the hang of it.

"Now" Faven said, "Close your eyes and imagine the colour you would like to manifest."
The girls closed their eyes and concentrated; Amelia excitedly opened her eyes first, as a golden glowing orb popped into existence floating just above the palm of her hand, quickly followed by Julia giggling as her bright pink orb appeared.
They looked at each other and smiled, pleased at their accomplishment.
"Well done" praised Faven, "Now we must rest, I bid you both a restful night."
"How do we stop the orbs Faven?" Asked Julia a note of urgency in her voice.
"Simply reverse the hand gestures, good night."

Amelia and Julia hugged each other good night and strolled to their tents guided by the light of their orbs.
As she drifted off to sleep Amelia's mind reeled a little from what she'd been able to accomplish that day. Maybe her and Julia really were meant to save this realm after all.
The reality of their quest to re-awaken this realms magic was beginning to feel a little less dreamlike.

When the following morning arrived, bathing the lands in its warming light, Amelia and Julia were both awoken by the suns rays illuminating them in the soft colourful hues of their tents luxurious materials.
Amelia opened her ornate chest, curious to know what was inside, as she did her eyes were met with a variety of new clothes and footwear.
She quickly shouted to Julia,
"Julia! Are you awake? Open your chest!"

"Ta da!" Julia exclaimed bursting from her tent door, arms outstretched flamboyantly, "Way ahead of you, check me out!"

Amelia hurriedly slipped on a new outfit, discovering that it magically reshaped to her body, making it a perfect and comfortable fit. She rushed outside to see Julia.
'Wow, you look amazing!" Amelia exclaimed as she scanned Julia from head to toe.
"So do you!" replied Julia with a big smile.

Faven was already at the centre of their encampment graciously arranging trays of delicious smelling foods.
The girls ate and drank their fill then as quickly as it had appeared the encampment was packed away again on the sled.

The next several days were spent trekking to the Mirror Lakes, an eerie landscape of glassy pools reflecting the realms unfamiliar tri-mooned skies above.
In the middle of these smooth waters stood a variety of large obelisks, etched with elegantly flowing markings.

Amelia and Julia held hands and began wading out into the shallow waters.

As they walked, tiny underwater plants cushioned their steps and colourful little aquatic creatures swam around occasionally tickling their feet.
Reaching the nearest obelisk, they paused for a minute to admire this delightful underwater display, gazing at the mesmerising colours and movement of these tiny underwater plants and their lively inhabitants.

As they gazed into the sparklingly clear waters of the lake, something strange began to happen, the water was darkening.
Amelia stooped closer, staring intently as everything vanished from view, subdued in a smoky blackness.
A sudden piercing scream rang out!
She turned quickly to see a dark mist lurch up from lake and wrap around Julias leg and with a sudden jerk Julia was pulled onto her side and was being dragged across the shallow waters at speed, with spray almost engulfing her as she tossed and turned, fighting this menacing smoky tentacle.
Amelia felt panic lurch inside her, she shouted out to Julia at the top of her lungs then glanced at the waters which were now entirely blackened.
Amelia squinted in horror as two piercing eyes formed in the darkness beneath her and an ominous smoky face appeared in the gloom, staring directly at her, she could almost feel its seething anger, as its pupils blazed like the fiery maelstrom the guardians had shown them.

Faven cried out, “Amelia touch the obelisk!”
Amelia rallied herself and grasped hold of the closest obelisk.
Her palms immediately glowed intensely, making her gasp, one after another the markings on the obelisks illuminated with a lightening bright radiance, casting fingers of sparkling light in multiple directions.
Julia let out a shocked cheer as she spluttered and leapt to her feet, dripping from head to toe, jubilant and teary at the same time, clearly shaken and wondering what exactly had just happened.

The lake waters cleared under the brilliance of the obelisk’s lights.
“We are safe now.” calmed Faven.
“I saw a face!” exclaimed Amelia as she embraced a very damp and trembling Julia.

“What form did this face take?” asked Faven, her expression serious.

"It was smoky black with piercing eyes and its pupils! Its pupils looked just like the fiery pits of the maelstrom that Torin showed to us."

Faven's face creased into a grave expression at Amelia's description. She closed her luminous eyes and drew a slow breath before speaking.

"It is as we feared. The face you saw belongs to the Ashen King, one of the most dangerous entities our realm has ever known."
Faven's voice took on a distant, sorrowful tone as she delved into the history of their ancient foe.

"Centuries ago, he arose from the Maelstrom itself, formed into consciousness, a being created from its swirling malevolence, born of its fiery intentions."
"We know not what dark pact brought him into being, only that his purpose was to corrupt all he touched."

Amelia and Julia listened intently, their eyes widening.

"At first, the Ashen King moved in secret, whispers of his evil spreading slowly like a plague.
He twisted unwary minds with promises of power, amassing the Outcast armies.
When finally he revealed himself, it was at the head of a force that threatened to drown this land in unending night."

Faven's expression was pained, as if the memories still carried powerful emotions.

"Many brave souls were lost before he was finally defeated.
Our greatest united against him at the Battle of the Broken Peaks.
The skies burned for seven days and nights before he was cast down, screaming back into the Maelstrom, his remaining followers were scattered or imprisoned."

"In the aftermath, we rejoiced, believing the Ashen King was destroyed forever.

But it seems some vestige of him has endured, weakened yet resolute to one day rise again...and now, his scattered followers have sensed their master's return.
If left unchecked, he will rise again more terrible than before."

Faven placed a gentle hand on Amelias' and Julias' shoulders, meeting their eyes solemnly.

"You carry a heavy burden young ones, to face a force so ancient and malevolent.
But remember, light ever prevails over darkness.
Keep faith in your gifts and we shall aid you however we can."

Amelia nodded, her initial fear giving way to a steelier resolve, not only to help Favens people but so that she and Julia get could back home safely again!
"Together, you must find the courage to unravel the mystery of this foe's return and see him banished once more." Said Faven resolutely.
Julia gave Amelias' hand a supportive squeeze, Amelia nodded to Julia silently with a defiant glint in her eyes.

Faven stood poised for a moment; her frame silhouetted against the dusky sky.
Her silvery hair billowed gently in the warm breeze as she closed her glowing eyes, communing silently with the birds circling overhead.
Serenity emanated from her, like the peace found gazing upon a still mountain lake.
She opened her eyes and smiled,
"The restorative balance of your presence has not come a moment too soon!"

That evening, Faven led them to a hidden grove filled with a swirling pink mist.
She called it the Vapor Cove and said that it possessed restorative properties.

As they entered this crescent shaped grotto, Amelia could just make out its honeycombed walls, each indent housing a tiny pulsating crystal that glowed softly giving the mist its colour, she coughed on the sweet-smelling vapor.

Suddenly, ghostly figures appeared in the mist, visions of Amelia's parents and her younger brother, Cole.
Seeing their faces shocked Amelia and she felt a strong yearning to be back at home.
The vapor was letting her glimpse their world!
"Mum...Dad..." she called out desperately, but the apparitions faded.
Even the fleeting contact filled Amelia with renewed conviction to see her family again.

Emerging from the cove, Amelia spoke with a defiant determination.
"We have a realm to save, come morning time, let's just keep moving."
Julia agreed, adding. "The sooner we get this done the sooner we'll be back home again."

Faven smiled proudly, and the following day they ventured onward with renewed spirits.

Amelia focused on the people she loved, using them as inspiration to power through doubt and tiredness.
She would see them again once this strange task was completed.
Until then, this realm needed her, and Julia needed her.

CHAPTER 4

Inner Darkness

Over the following days, they travelled onward, the landscape shifting from dreary decay to vibrancy again as Amelia, assisted by Julia, restored beautiful lifegiving fountains that had ceased flowing, bringing fresh life back into parched groves, and imbuing all kinds of curious statuary with positive magical energy once again.
Each time, Amelia and Julia were able to channel their inner glow, rejuvenating the flow of magic just enough for it to take on a life of its own once again, and do the rest.
With each success, the Maelstrom's hold appeared to retreat, whilst the Realm of Reflections slowly began regaining its lustre.

Slowly but surely Amelia and Julia felt the pace of the quest taking its toll.
They were exhausted and Amelia felt the responsibility weighing on her.
Sensing her friend's stress, Julia tried boosting Amelia's morale with silly jokes and songs.
Amelia was grateful for the comfort, even forcing a few laughs.
But doubt still nagged at her.
What if they failed? What if these new abilities just stopped?
What if this was all some elaborate hoax or delusion?

Yet the events of the recent days made it harder to deny the supernatural truth that was unfolding before them.

As another evening closed in, the trio made camp near the bend of a tranquil river.
The sun began setting over the glistening waters; Faven tended to a warming fire whilst Amelia sat pensively staring at the gently flickering flames.
"Your powers are growing stronger," Faven said, glancing at Amelia lost in her thoughts.
"I can sense the light within you both shining brighter than ever."

Amelia managed a faint smile.

"I guess so. I still don't really understand what's happening when we revive those shrines and monuments. It just...flows through me."
Julia gave her an encouraging nudge.
"Don't overthink it! Just keep working the magic. We're totally winning."

But Amelia couldn't shake her lingering doubts.
Were her abilities even real? Or was this all some vivid dream?
The weight of responsibility on her shoulders felt so stressful.

That night, Amelia had vivid nightmares of the magical realm plunging into darkness, overwhelmed by the malevolent Ashen King and the Maelstrom.
She saw her family and friends back home suffering too.
Amelia cried out but couldn't stop the darkness from consuming everything.
She awoke with a gasp, shaking uncontrollably.
Julia rushed over, looking worried.
"Whoa, just breathe! What's going on?"

Amelia recounted her nightmare, tears welling up.
"What if I can't stop the darkness? What if I fail and let everyone down?"
Julia gripped her shoulders firmly.
"Hey, we can do this together. Don't stress about the what-ifs. Just take it one day at a time."

Her words helped to sooth Amelia's anxiety and soon enough, sleep was upon them once more.

As dawn broke, they resumed their journey toward the next site, the Caverns of Whispers.
Amelia steeled herself, determined not to let her doubts sabotage their mission.

However, when they arrived at the caverns entrance, a wave of claustrophobia struck her.
The rocky tunnels stretching into endless blackness filled Amelia with a primal dread.

Noticing her hesitation, Faven touched her shoulder gently.
"The caves represent facing your inner darkness. But your light truly can overcome any shadows here."

Amelia took a deep breath. She had to conquer this fear.
With Julia grasping her hand, they ventured into the caves.
Amelia conjured an orb of light to guide them through the gloom.

As they went deeper, eerie whispers echoed around them.
Amelia strained to make out words, but they remained elusive.
The hairs on her neck prickled as the whispers grew more insistent.

"Turn back...imposter...you're not welcome here...you're weak...failure is assured..." the disembodied voices jibed.

Amelia faltered, the haunting words striking deep at her innermost doubts.
Sensing her distress, Julia squeezed her hand reassuringly.

"Don't listen to those lies," she said firmly.
"You're brave and growing more powerful by the day. We can do this."

Bolstered by her friend's confidence, Amelia pressed on until the narrow tunnel opened into a huge cavern.
Before them stood a towering demonic smoke being, it grinned menacingly as if lit by inner fire. Tendrils of red light snaked through the cavern, accompanied by a rush of scorching wind.

The Maelstrom was here, fighting back.

Amelia's long hair lashed her face as she stumbled backward, startled by what she was seeing, the entity's voice rose to deafening screams in her mind, promising failure and misery.

She angrily fought to ignore the words but it felt so much like being back at all those schools she'd endured, sly comments and hurtful sneers pelting her like rain, she felt alone and insignificant.

Suddenly she was aware of Julia grasping her shoulders,
"Fight!" Julia screamed.
Amelia focused every ounce of her inner light.
"I am not that person; I am kind and caring and I can beat this craziness!"

In unison the girls began to state aloud the good deeds that they had already accomplished, they focused on their loved ones and the utmost importance of this quest.
Their entire bodies began to glow brighter and brighter until in a powerful crescendo, a wave of pure energy pulsed from their bodies, cascading through the caves, forcing out the dark apparition.

Panting hard her heart racing, Amelia jumped to her feet.
Julia let out a cry of delight and hugged her ecstatically.

"You did it! I knew you could overcome the darkness," she gushed.
“We did it!” replied Amelia beaming with a relieved smile.

The soothing golden light from her orb was all that now remained, illuminating the empty cavern around them.

Exiting the caves triumphantly, Amelia felt her confidence soar.
The malicious whispers had shown her, that she possessed true inner strength, that her inner light could never be extinguished by doubt.
Faven congratulated them warmly.

Their journey was far from over.
But with her friends beside her and new belief in herself, Amelia felt she could shine brighter now, no matter the depths of the darkness they may face ahead.

CHAPTER 5

Ripples of Kindness

After leaving the Cavern of Whispers behind they camped once more near the river bend, getting some days of welcome rest.

After a deep and pleasant sleep, Amelia and Julia woke early, deciding to head for a swim in the nearby river.

“This river is known for its mystical waters,” Faven called to the girls as they left.

The rivers surface shimmered with an iridescent glow as they approached the edge, and the air became charged with a subtle, magical energy.
Amelia could feel it tingling on her skin, a sensation like a gentle caress from the river's aura.
"Isn't it beautiful?" Julia gasped; her eyes wide with wonder.
"It's breathtaking," Amelia agreed, her heart beginning to flutter with excitement.

They approached a secluded spot where the river widened into a small pool, framed by lush wildflower meadow and overhanging trees that dappled the area with patches of light.

The waters beckoned them, and without hesitation, they shed their clothes and stepped into the refreshing embrace of the magical river.

As soon as they entered the water, a delightful sensation enveloped them. The river's magic was alive and welcoming, swirling around their bodies, it seemed to respond to their presence, creating tiny ripples that danced along the surface of their skin with every movement they made.

Amelia and Julia laughed joyously as they splashed and swam in the river.

The water was surprisingly buoyant, and felt as if it was cradling them, enabling them to effortlessly float along its leisurely currents.

"Look at this!" Amelia exclaimed, cupping her hands together and lifting them out of the water.
In her palms, a cluster of water droplets had formed, each one rolling on her palms and glimmering like tiny gems.
She blew gently on them, and they scattered into the air floating momentarily, before disappearing back into the river.

Julia was not to be outdone. She playfully dipped her fingers into the water and drew intricate patterns, leaving behind trails of sparkling light that twinkled like the stars back home.

As Amelia and Julia waded into the shallows, a timid creature emerged from the trees on the riverbank. It resembled a delicate fawn with large dark eyes and small budding antlers, but had a short cute trunk like an elephant.

The fawn sniffed the air curiously but kept its distance, watching the girls with wary fascination.

"It's okay, you can come say hi," Julia said gently, slowly wading toward the shore.
She held out her hand, allowing the skittish fawn creature to catch her scent.

After several hesitant moments, its courage grew.
The fawn stepped forward, extending its snout and blowing a sudden spray of water at the delighted girls!

Once the initial surprise wore off, Amelia and Julia laughed joyously.
The fawn seemed pleased by their reaction and continued shooting water at them playfully.

"I think someone wants to be friends," Amelia grinned, smoothing the fawn's velvety fur when it finally drew near.
Gaining more confidence, the endearing creature ventured into the shallows, paddling beside them on its spindly legs.
It stayed close, allowing the girls to stroke its head and scratch behind its tufted ears.

After a heartwarming few minutes swimming together, the fawn bleated fondly before leaving the water and frolicking back into the lush forest.

Amelia and Julia waved a wistful goodbye, warmed by the innocent joy and companionship of their new woodland friend.

As they continued to explore the magical properties of the river, they noticed something extraordinary happening.
The water around them began to wash away their doubts and fears, leaving them feeling more connected, not only to one another but also to this magical realm itself that they found themselves destined to save.

The following morning, they were up early and packed, ready to go.

With no time to waste, Faven led them toward a new part of the realm.

“This place ahead is known as the Valley of Sighs.” she told them as they walked together eventually entering the new terrain.

As they descended into a vast valley, no birdsong nor insects could be heard. Thick grey fog obscured their vision until a sad, sweet melody echoed through the haze.

"Beware the sorrowful energy here," Faven warned.
"Many fall prey to despair in this place."

They pushed onward, guided by the mournful music.
Soon, shadowy figures appeared wandering aimlessly, their woeful sighs harmonising with the melancholy chorus.
Amelia's heart ached for these lost souls.
"What happened to them?" she asked Faven.
Faven shook her head sadly.
"They surrendered their joy and hope to the Maelstrom's clutches. Now they feed its power with their misery.
We fear that the Ashen King is attempting to spread his malevolent maelstrom as far and wide across the realms as he is able, transmogrifying its nourishing magic and twisting it to his own evil ends."

Before too long they reached the music's source, a faded pavilion where a lone pianist sat before faded ivory keys. The notes resonating the sorrow of the valley's misfortune.

Amelia cautiously approached the pianist whose fingers continued playing the woeful tune.
Meeting the figure's sunken gaze, she implored,
"Your music is so beautiful. Please don't squander it on despair."

The pianist halted abruptly, appearing stunned by her words.

The grey fog swirled faster, forming into monstrous shapes, accompanied by shrieks as the Maelstrom resisted losing its disconsolate minions.

Laying her hands gently atop the worn-out piano keys, Amelia delved through her memories.
She recalled songs from her favourite albums, tunes she'd danced to and favourite songs she'd mastered on her beloved guitar, even a lullaby her mum had sang to her as a child, all helping her to amplify the positive energy she now felt welling up inside.

Like a flower in springtime the instruments faded colours began brightening until the keys and woodwork gleamed anew.
Soon joyful music rang out, echoing around the valley and dispelling the oppressive fog.
The shadowy wanderers blinked in confusion as the gloom in their souls lifted and the valley began to transform.

That evening they stayed as guests of the valleys' inhabitants.
The locals wishing to show their appreciation, held an impromptu celebration for Amelia, Julia, and Faven, immeasurably grateful for the trio's kind efforts in lifting the valley's despair.

All manner of tables and chairs were brought out into the streets and stacked high with delectable food and drink.
Colourful bunting and banners were hung between buildings, and Faven added a variety of magical glowing orbs to light up the festivities.

Musicians played lively songs, and everyone danced joyfully late into the night.
Amelia and Julia danced until their feet ached, revelling in the valley folks' regained hope and cheer.

When the first light of dawn peeked over the ridgeline, the thoroughly exhausted but elated trio retired to soft beds where a deep and restorative sleep ensued.

CHAPTER 6

The Resistance

After hugging many of their new friends and wishing them all well, they left the now rejuvenating slopes of the valley behind and ventured on.
After walking together for some time, the terrain ahead grew more treacherous as Faven acting as guide began ascending sheer cliff pathways.
Soon Amelia and Julia found themselves having to brave a biting wind as Faven led them across a dangerously old bridge that spanned a rocky chasm, finally stopping at the mouth of a craggy looking cave entrance.

"An Oracle resides within." Said Faven.
"Ask for guidance and if she favours you, her advice could prove invaluable."

Amelia and Julia crawled through the narrow cave opening, strange glyphs on the walls began to glow, illuminating their path until the tunnel opened into a glittering grotto.

Seated beside a small crackling fire was a figure concealed in tattered robes. She slowly lifted her hood, revealing a beautiful but careworn face with striking violet eyes.

"Greetings Amelia and Julia," she rasped in a soft, lilting voice.
"The oracle Ethaine welcomes you. Your light shines bold and bright."

Uneasily, Amelia asked,
"What guidance do you have for us?"

The mysterious oracle beckoned them closer.
"Come...come young ones, your presence here is welcome, come warm yourselves by this fire.
Heed my guidance.
You both possess more potential than you yet realise.

But... to defeat the Ashen King and his multifarious followers, you will require more than this newly acquired magic you're learning.
You must build an army of the realm... a resistance!
Begin by seeking out the sky folk then the woodland clans."

And with that, Ethaine retreated back into her hood.
“Mustn't linger.” was her parting comment.

Amelia and Julia hurriedly left the cave and re-met with Faven, sharing with her the oracles advice.

"You must head for Stormvale first and make peace with the tempestuous sky beings," she advised. "Their flying steeds are revered throughout the realm."

It took several more days crossing over rugged peaks before they finally reached Stormvale, a city carved into the mountainside itself.
Hundreds of winged humanoids glided overhead among the cloudy spires.

A sceptical envoy approached them and after some abrupt discourse agreed to escort Amelia, Julia and Faven to have an audience with their severe queen.
"Make your plea but choose your words wisely," he warned.
"Queen Visoo suffers no fools."

In the sparse mountain throne room, the imposing queen sat draped in luxurious robes, flanked by two fearsome winged guards.
"Why have you come uninvited to my kingdom, humans?" she demanded.

Remaining outwardly composed, Amelia diplomatically asked for the queen's aid against the Ashen King and his maelstrom, proposing an alliance.
The queen sat impassively for several agonizing moments; her gaze fixed unflinchingly upon the girls.

Finally, she nodded.
"Your quest is noble. We too have suffered the darkness encroaching on our lands.
Stormvale will join this resistance."

Amelia and Julia bowed respectfully, feeling inwardly delighted.
The days that followed their audience with Queen Visoo were intense and transformative.

Amelia and Julia integrated themselves into the daily life of Stormvale, meeting the sky folk and sharing stories with the winged citizens.
They spent time learning to ride their magnificent, winged mounts.
Amelia to her surprise found that she enjoyed seeing the realm from such exhilarating heights and forming a deep bond with such powerful yet gentle animals.
The sky folk's way of life was vastly different from their own, and yet, amidst the clouds and spires, a sense of unity and purpose prevailed with their newfound allies.

During their daily interactions, they overheard a worrying rumour.
The queen's son, Prince Erevan, had very recently been captured by a rogue faction from the peaks of Stormvale, known as the Tempest Brotherhood.
These rebels sought to align with the dark energies of the maelstrom for their own nefarious purposes.
"Well, this certainly explains the queen's fearsome demeanour." Said Amelia.
"We should offer our help," she added, shrugging her shoulders at Julia and Faven.
"Without hesitation," agreed Julia nodding.

The trio arranged another meeting with queen Visoo who confirmed the rumours and revealed to them that she was currently torn between the love for her son and her duty to her people.
"I fear starting an all-out war should I attack the Tempest Brotherhood," stated the queen.
"We don't yet know the size of their dark ally's army.
My scouts have tracked down the rebel encampment and are gathering information about my sons situation as we speak, they will be returning soon.
The rebels have not yet made any demands." The queen continued,
"Which bodes well for us, it is indicative that their malevolent allies have not yet been informed of my sons capture, which provides us with a short window of time to act."

Amelia, Julia and Faven offered their aid, suggesting that they would not be associated with her Kingdom should they be caught.
The queen seemed taken aback back this valiant offer and after some thought she accepted.
"Once my scouts have returned, we will furnish your requirements, our swiftest black steeds, camouflaged attire and several of my elite guards at your service."

As night fell, guided by the knowledge that the Stormvale scouts had conveyed, they devised a plan for a stealthy rescue.

Under the cover of night, they embarked on their journey through turbulent skies, finally arriving at the hidden fortress' perimeter, nestled amongst storm choked canyons.
Thunder rumbled and flashes of intermittent lightening created ominous looking shadows upon the canyons rock face.
They approached the fortress high up in the air, their movements masked by the winds and rumbling thunder.

Onward they flew until they'd passed over the outer walls, finally coming to a hover, high above the strongholds maze like interior.
"Quickly now!" urged queen Visoos elite guards, "whilst it is clear below."
They dropped three black cords that contained climbing knots along their lengths and secured them to the saddles of Amelia, Julia and Favens hovering steeds.
Amelia took a breath and began her descent, climbing down the rope into the darkness, she could feel it swaying in the winds.
The others followed, Julia's nerves had gotten the better of her and she felt herself trembling as she dismounted and began climbing down the rope, grasping it tightly with each careful movement.

Amelia reached the floor and glanced up into the blackness.
At that moment a fork of brilliant lighting snaked across the stormy skies, enabling her a brief glimpse of the group silhouetted against the storming skies.
Above, the same fork of lightening had caused Julia's steed to lurch suddenly before correcting its flight.
The sudden movement travelled down Julia's rope like a whip crack.

She gasped as her grip broke free; it took all of her will not to scream as she twisted around dangling in mid-air, clinging on for dear life with her one remaining hand.
What seemed like an eternity of panic was but a split second as Faven reached across, firmly placing Julia's flailing hand back onto the rope.

Together they reached Amelia on the ground, Julia could feel her heart and mind racing.
"This way." Asserted Faven without moving her lips, her voice was as clear as a bell inside the girls' heads, they glanced at one another momentarily then quickly followed her as she led, slipping through narrow passageways and hidden alcoves.

At several corners they could see dancing silhouettes, shadows cast from the glowing fires, where members of the Tempest Brotherhood stood guard.
As they reached the heart of the fortress, a location that the queens scouts had indicated Prince Erevan was being held, they spotted a lone Guard.
Directly behind the guard, a large floating cage hung in air, its bars hummed and crackled with energy and imprisoned within, asleep on the cage floor, was the queens son.

Amelia and Julia communicated through subtle gestures and eye contact, silently coordinating their actions whilst they continued to hear Favens voice speaking clearly in their heads.
Faven explained that she could encapsulate the guard within a cylinder of illusion, manipulating his view, he would continue to see his surroundings unchanged and though he would not be able to see the girls, he would still be able to hear them, so they must move silently under the cover of the nights storm.

The trio crouched low and silently inched their way closer to the floating cage.
They stopped as near as they dare to the crackling bars and viewed the lock.
Its appearance was confusing and like nothing the girls had ever seen before.
It looked like a metallic scroll etched with unusual ornate writings.

"This is an ancient Lock," Amelia and Julia heard Faven explain.
"It is a riddle; you must whisper the one correct answer for it to open.
If the wrong answer is given the cage will be forever sealed."

Amelia clasped her hand over her mouth to prevent her from blurting out the exasperation she was feeling.

"I shall interpret the riddle," Faven continued:

'In realms where stars their light do spill,
A forest deep, where dreams distil.
With brilliance bathed in daylight's grace,
A precious seed, from nature's love.

Delicate in form, hues so bright,
In summers blooming, pure delight.
Yet heed you must, for thorns do live,
A touch amiss, they'll not forgive.

Love's emblem true, by all adored,
From natures ground, pure ore is poured.
In lyrics of songs to legends told,
And history's tales, there I've glowed.

So, seeker wise, now heed my call,
What might I be, enchanting all?
A flowering riddle, secrets unfold,
The answer gleams...'

Julia met Amelias eye excitedly, she cupped her hands around Amelias ear and quickly whispered.
"I know it, I know it...it's a flower... no wait a rose, a rose, it's a rose!"
"No, it can't be that simple," thought Amelia.

She indicated to Faven to read them the riddle again and then again.
Upon Favens third reading, Julias face lit up, she whispered to Julia who nodded in strong agreement. Faven also gave her nod of approval.

Amelia moved her lips as close as she dared toward the dangerous crackling energy of the lock and whispered her answer.
"A rose of gold." She mouthed almost silently.
Nothing happened, Amelias heart sank, fearing she had entombed the prince for all eternity, and now they would have to face the angry wrath of the queen.

Then suddenly, with a surge of power the cage door swung open with a hum, they all froze as the nearby guard shifted on his feet and glanced towards them.

Prince Erevan opened his eyes and surveyed his female rescuers suspiciously.

They gestured to the prince to remain silent and beckoned him to follow them as they hurriedly retraced their steps through the darkened fortress, the storm still raging overhead.
Sweat was beading on their foreheads as they avoided patrols within this labyrinth of danger, each step bringing them closer to the freedom of the ropes and awaiting steeds.

Finally reaching the right place they frantically grasped the ropes and began climbing, only to feel their strength waning.
Mercifully the queens strong guards quickly hoisted them up, seating them back into their saddles.
In a sudden flurry of wing strokes, the powerful steeds were off, flying at speed through the wind and into the blackness of the night.
Storm clouds roiled and crashed among the rugged peaks, thunder echoing across the vast chasms below.

Jagged forks of lightning rent the gloom, flashing amid the mountain rain.

Through the chaos flew the sky folk, their steeds' wings unfurling powerfully, never more in their element than when racing nature's violent majesty. Amelia and Julias emotions felt as turbulent as the storms and they hung on tightly.

Mercifully they finally arrived back safely into Stormvale.
Standing out in the storm with her personal guard, Queen Visoo awaited their return.
Reunited, the queen and her son the prince embraced, their tears of joy mingling with the storms rains.

Immeasurably grateful for the courage and loyalty Amelia, Julia, and Faven had shown, Queen Visoo called for a grand ceremony to be held the very next day.
The rescue group embraced one another.
"We of the Sky Guard Salute you!" spoke the queens elite, their hands symbolically pressed against their hearts, they bowed low then slipped away into the nights shadows.

The following day a huge assembly of Sky Folk had gathered in the great square, flanked by the majestic spires of the mountain range, Queen Visoo stepped forward, her wings spread wide.

"My honoured guests, I owe you an unrepayable debt of gratitude."
Prince Erevan stepped forward presenting them, one by one, with an exotic and intricate amulet, each adorned with a swirling storm pattern.

"These amulets are relics of our people," continued the queen, "They were imbued with powerful magical essences long ago, accept them as a token of gratitude for your incredible selfless aid.
These amulets will infuse with your own powers," the queen intoned, her voice carrying weight. "With them, you will wield the strength of storms, and your connection to our realm will remain unbreakable."

Amelia, Julia, and Faven stood shoulder to shoulder accepting their amulets with proud smiles, Amelia glanced at Julia as a shiver of delight coursed

through her body, her heart full of appreciation for the friendships they had forged and the unity they had achieved.
As they fastened the amulets around their necks, a surge of energy flowed through them, a powerful reminder of the bonds they'd formed and the challenges they'd overcome.

With joyful hearts, the trio now looked ahead to their next destination, the lush Verdant Forest, where they hoped to recruit the diverse woodland beings who inhabited that realm.

Upon their arrival in the forests, they found a vibrant community of woodland creatures thriving in harmony with the ancient trees and lush nature.

The leader of the woodland realm was Mursuh, a wise and muscular centaur with a chestnut horse body and rugged human torso. He welcomed them warmly to the heart of the forest village.
"Of course we will join forces with you! The maelstrom and its perpetrator of destruction must be stopped."

The diverse woodland clans lived together in a sprawling village of moss-covered stone cottages interspersed with massive hollowed out tree trunks serving as communal halls and homes.

Centaurs were the protectors and warriors, possessing powerful horse-like lower bodies and strong human torsos, wielding swords and bows.
There were also many nimble satyrs, whose sturdy goat legs allowed them to traverse the forest's rocky crags with ease. Their horns were adorned with vines and leaves, and many rode large antlered stags as mounts.

Pixies fluttered through the branches, their delicate wings leaving trails of fine glittering dust on the foliage.
Elvish musicians played haunting melodies on hand carved instruments, their songs echoing through the trees.

That evening a great feast was held, with all manner of nuts, berries and roasted vegetables.

Mead and berry wines flowed freely as all danced together under the stars and moons around a roaring bonfire. Tales were told late into the night of the forest's rich history and myths.

The following days were filled with intensive training, as Amelia and Julia learned to ride sleek stags through the lush forest glades.

Their centaur allies instructed them in archery, gifting them enchanted bows made of polished ironbark that amplified the force and aim of the shooter. When drawn, the bowstrings thrummed with latent power.

For close combat, they were presented with elegant swords forged by the satyrs from rare metals mined deep underground. Runes etched along the blades allowed them to channel natural magic, so they hummed and glowed when wielded.

The forest folk taught Amelia and Julia their fighting techniques passed down through generations. They learned to duck and roll gracefully alongside their stag mounts and strike with enhanced speed and precision with their new weapons.

During their scarce moments of respite from the rigorous training, the forest folk would lead Amelia and Julia in meditative communion with the ancient towering trees, teaching them to open their minds and draw upon the vital energy of nature's magic that coursed through their vibrant realm.

Sitting crossed-legged upon the knotted roots, they would close their eyes and slow their breathing, working to find stillness amidst the sounds of the thriving forest.
Focusing their awareness, they reached out with their feelings, striving to connect with the ancient wisdom and primal power dwelling within the colossal trunks and burrowing roots.

When their minds quieted, Amelia and Julia could sense the trees' latent magic, an enduring, patient energy that waxed and waned with the seasons. The wise centaurs instructed them to respectfully invite this energy in, guiding it through their bodies and spirits.
The energy swelled and subsided within them like a gentle tide as their consciousness intertwined with the spirits of the great trees.

With practice, drawing upon the natural magic grew easier.
Amelia and Julia learned to tap into its restorative currents whenever exhaustion overcame them.
In time, it flowed through them as steadily as sap coursing through the towering trunks and branches surrounding them.
Though much training still lay ahead, they were beginning to harness the intrinsic magic of the Verdant Forest.
Amelia and Julia bonded profoundly with the diverse forest clans during their days of magical training and combat drills.
They both felt immensely grateful for the help and kindnesses that had been lavished upon them, gracing them with a greater sense of readiness to tackle whatever lay ahead.

United with these powerful new allies, their company finally set out with them to return to Stormvale and plan their next move.
The resistance had been built, but would it be enough?

That night Amelia confessed her lingering self-doubt to Julia.
" We've come so far but I'm terrified of actually confronting the Ashen King and his followers."

Julia forced a smile.
"Hey, we're all scared. But you don't have to carry this alone anymore. We're in this together and with help from the realm too."

Comforted, Amelia tried to sleep, but her mind kept playing out catastrophic scenarios.
She knew the final confrontation with the Ashen King would happen all too soon, whether they were ready or not.

At sunrise, Faven urgently shook them.
"Rise quickly! We must go!
The Ashen King and his minions have come forth from their hiding, they've launched a direct attack!"

Stepping outside, Amelia gasped to see the sky swallowed by malevolent dark clouds.

In the distance, armies of shadowy beasts marched forward on a sea of molten flame, corrupting everything they touched.

Faven turned to the girls, her expression grave.
"We cannot delay any longer. It is time. We make our stand!"

With their allies assembled, Amelia and Julia rode to the front, Amelia mounted on a magnificent white winged charger and Julia at her side riding a great Stag.
Both girls wore their treasures of the realm, the powerful amulets adorned around their necks to amplify their magic.
Though her heart was pounding with fear, Amelia held her head high.

The Ashen King and his hordes awaited.
"I will not faulter with so many counting on me". She thought, steadying her nerves.

As they prepared to battle for the fate of the realm, Amelia summoned every ounce of her courage.

The final confrontation was here.
Light would face off against dark.
And she would help them to triumph, no matter the cost!

CHAPTER 7

Battle of Wills

Amelia and Julia rode at the head of the resistance, flanked on both sides by Mursuh and Visoo.
Ahead the looming legions of the Maelstrom were moving ever closer.
Hideous shadow beasts stalked the barren valley ahead, sent as the vanguard of their forces.

"Well, this is another crazy adventure we've gotten ourselves into," Amelia said, wiping away a tear. "But with you here, I think we'll be just fine."
Julia let out a laugh and nodded, her whole-body trembling, her expression turning serious again. "We've got this Amelia. Just like always."
She leaned over and hugged Amelia.
No matter what happened next, their bond was unbreakable.

Drawing their mystical blades the girls exchanged resolute nods before charging forward on their beasts.
The troops of the resistance shouted with defiant zeal and surged forth into the fray.

The vale echoed with snarls and screams as the two sides collided.
Guided by pure instinct, Amelia hacked and slashed through the foul beasts, her sword cutting with a blazing energy, leaving nothing but floating ash in its wake.

All around, their allies fought bravely.
The burly centaurs trampled swaths of monsters beneath their powerful hooves whilst airborne Stormvale archers expertly rained down magical arrows onto their enemies.

Satyrs worked in tight formation, interlocking their hexagonal shields and wielding imbued axes that glowed as they swung them with ferocity, reaving their way deeper into the enemy hordes.

Light footed elves moved with dance like grace amidst the silvery blur of their elegantly crafted swords.
For a moment it seemed they had gained the advantage.
But as more dark creatures poured into the valley, the Resistance began to falter.

Amelia rallied, refusing to give in to despair.
"For the Realm of Reflections!" she cried, raising her blade.
With a resounding chant the resistance surged forward.

Amelia spotted Faven clashing fiercely with several monstrous shadow hounds.
Spurring her steed, she took flight, soaring at speed to aid Faven before one of the beasts could pounce from behind.
As her steed swooped down landing squarely between the shadow hound and Faven, Amelia's sword hummed through the air in a scything arc, it struck true, felling the hound in a single motion, leaving nothing but ash floating on the breeze.

"My thanks!" gasped Faven, nodding graciously.
"The battle tilts dangerously. We must finish this!"
Back-to-back, the two cleaved through the smouldering horde, Julia joined them, her stag hurling enemies across the battlefield with its antlers, as they valiantly carved a path toward the king.

Amelia and Julia as one began unleashing blasts of pure light, decimating swathes of creatures that surrounded them.
The Resistance cheered at the sight of the three of them, their morale soaring.

But the gruelling battle was taking its toll.
Wounded warriors lay strewn across the battlefield.
Amelia knew they needed to reach the King before all was lost.

As they fought on, the Ashen king loomed before them, pulsing with malevolence, his smouldering eyes fixed upon them.
Drawing on every last ounce of energy, Amelia and Julia unleashed the magic stored within their artifacts.

Resplendent streaks of lightning erupted forth, spearing toward the dark heart of the King.
The landscape trembled under the collision of the opposing forces.
With teeth clenched, the girls poured everything they had into their attack.
"You shall not win!" Amelia yelled in defiant desperation.
The Kings abyss seemed bottomless, resisting their pure light.
But slowly, the darkness began fraying at its edges.

With a deafening roar, the Ashen king violently imploded then exploded into a giant fiery sphere, ejecting the girls backward. Amelia's head slammed down hard.
Dazed, she forced her eyes open to see the dust settling over the valley.

The Ashen king, his minions and the maelstrom had vapourised and nothing but smouldering ashes remained floating slowly to the ground.
They had won! A huge cheer rang out across the battlefield.

Amelia, Julia and Faven stood panting, surveying the aftermath, the victory had come at a grave price.
All around, Resistance soldiers lay unmoving alongside the smouldering ash outlines of monstrosities.
Survivors, some limping, moved about the battlefield tending the wounded.

So much sacrifice thought Amelia mournfully. So many allies and new friends were lost.
The realm was saved but at great cost.

Late into the night, the dead were honoured and the injured tended to.

The following day felt solemn as a convoy of Skyguards flew Amelia and Julia back to Favens sprawling crystalline home city.

Upon the approach of their arrival, trumpets sounded to mark their return.
Amelia and Julias feelings were bittersweet, tinged with grief for those not there to share in the triumph.
A great evil had been defeated, yet losses weighed heavily on the victors.

As feasts and celebrations were held, Amelia grappled with her inner turmoil.
Lives had been the cost of her destiny.

What if she had found another way? The guilt choked her.

Sensing her friend's sorrow, Julia tried consoling her.
"Because of you, the darkness won't keep spreading. Don't let survivor's guilt consume you."

Amelia managed a small, grateful smile but the festivities still felt somewhat hollow to her.
Her head was swimming.
When would the portal reopen for them to finally go home?
She desperately needed her family's comfort and a sense of normality.

As a new morning dawned, Amelia walked with Julia through the mystic grove, talking of all that had taken place.
As they strolled, Faven approached, accompanied by the guardians.
“It is time” said Torin with a smile.
“The energy is restoring and rebalancing, we are indebted to you.”

“Farewell my courageous sisters, it has been such a great honour,” said Faven, cupping both their hands in her own.
She then lightly placed her hand onto a symbol etched into the archway to the side of the path on which they stood.
The carved symbol lit up with sudden radiance.
Amelia and Julia stepped back a little as the air inside the archway began to shimmer and coalesce into a whirling portal!
It was reopened at last!
Joy and trepidation gripped Amelia's heart.
Their epic quest here was completed.

Steeling themselves, the girls teary eyed stepped into the portal's embrace.
A kaleidoscope of light enveloped their senses and for a brief moment they both felt weightless.

CHAPTER 8

An Uneasy Return

Amelia stumbled out of the portal and sank to her knees in the dirt, overcome with relief to be back in her own world.
Julia emerged behind her, looking equally drained but flashing a weary smile.

"We made it," she breathed, helping Amelia to her feet.
After joyfully embracing, they walked slower than usual until they reached the neighbourhood park, settling on the swings it all came flooding out, the dizzying highs, crushing lows, wonders and terrors.

"It's crazy no time passed here," Julia said.
"We saved a whole realm but on Earth it's just another school day ending."

Amelia nodded, her mind still struggling to process everything.
One moment she had been a shy new student eating alone. The next, a saviour, wielding magic on an epic quest.

"Do you think the portal will ever reopen?" Julia asked.

Amelia sighed, slowly rocking her swing.
"I'm not sure. I hope we can go back someday."

Returning home, Amelia's mum greeted her with a hug.
"How was class today? Make any new friends?"

Amelia managed a tired smile.
"You could say that." She couldn't even begin to explain her unbelievable alternate "school day."

Upstairs, Amelia collapsed gratefully onto her bed. Her hands falling to rest on the storm amulet Queen Visoo had bestowed her, memories of the winged allies flooded her mind and exhilarated her heart.
She thought of the incredible adventures shared with both Faven and Julia. In the Realm of Reflections, she had found somewhere she belonged, a place where she felt that she fit, even if only for a short time.

The following days at school were easier.
Amelia walked the halls with a new confidence, no longer feeling like the timid new girl.

Each morning she eagerly flung open her wardrobe and planned her outfit, embracing clothing as a way to show her true self, wearing outfits she would have been too shy and insecure to wear previously.
She started dressing more boldly in a style that expressed her adventurous spirit.
Gone were the muted hoodies and plain jeans. In their place, she embraced flowing skirts that swirled with every step and colourful tops that she also paired with ripped jeans.

Amelia organised her once hidden collection of jewellery.
Chunky bracelets jingling merrily with each movement and an array of earrings became an extension of her being, symbolizing the layers of courage she had uncovered within herself.

She even began experimenting with some new edgy makeup, dark eyeliner and lipsticks in a variety of different shades.
Wearing these trendy clothes made Amelia feel more like the brave, magical heroine she had become.
She no longer feared drawing attention and carried herself differently; instead, her new look sparked several conversations and comments of admiration.

Amelia strolled into the crowded cafeteria; head held high. For once, she didn't duck into the first empty table she saw. Striding up to a group of stylish girls she recognized from her math class, she smiled.

"Hey! Mind if I join you guys today?"

The girls looked surprised but nodded eagerly, making space at their table. As Amelia sat down, she noticed several nearby students glancing her way, as if suddenly seeing her in a new light.

"Love your outfit, Amelia! Where did you get that top?" said Megan, one of the math girls.

"Thanks! I found it at this cool vintage shop in town over the weekend," Amelia said, enjoying the opportunity to talk fashion.

As they chatted, Amelia was conscious of people checking her out. A group of boys at the next table kept stealing glances at her in between their conversations.
It gave Amelia a thrill of confidence.

The math girls turned out to be really nice and invited Amelia to sit with them the next day too.
As she grabbed her tray to leave, Amelia noticed a guy named Nathan she recognized from English class eyeing her bold new makeup.

"Hey Amelia, cool eye makeup," he said. "It looks awesome on you."

"Thanks Nathan!" she replied cheerfully. "Just trying something new with my look."

As she walked to history, she noticed several other students she didn't know saying hi and giving her friendly smiles.

Amelia grinned, holding her head high. In such a short time, her new style had transformed how her peers saw her.
She felt admired, included...even a bit popular. This school didn't seem so scary anymore.

Julia too seemed transformed, practically floating through the halls of her school, entranced by her new boyfriend Callum!
Amelia was thrilled to see Julia glowing with joy after she had sparked a conversation with Callum and just outright asked him on a date.

She and Callum had really hit it off on their first date at the pizza place in town.
Now they were officially boyfriend and girlfriend!
Julia still got butterflies remembering their first kiss outside of her front door.

As she headed to her locker, she saw Callum down the hall talking with some guys from the football team. He caught her eye and waved, his cute dimples making Julia blush.

"I'll text you later Jules!" he called out, before continuing his conversation.
Julia smiled and gave a small wave back, noticing some girls nearby shooting her envious looks.

She knew Callum was considered a major hottie. Other girls gossiped about his tousled black hair, deep brown eyes and athletic physique. But Julia was the one who worked up the nerve to talk to him.

At lunch, Julia sat with Callum and his new friends.
Under the table, Callum held her hand, stroking his thumb over her skin.
“You look really pretty today,” he whispered in her ear. Julia’s heart did somersaults.

As they all joked and chatted, she realized how comfortable she felt already with Callum.
He made her laugh with his goofy jokes. And when he smiled at her, she felt like the luckiest girl in school.

After lunch as they walked to history, Callum suddenly pulled her into a small alcove in the hallway and kissed her, Julia melted into his arms, all thoughts vanishing except how crazy she was about him.

When the bell rang, they rushed to class grinning and holding hands. Julia was so happy that she’d found someone that saw how special she was.
With Callum by her side, she knew this term would be amazing.

The first several weeks, being back home felt blissful to Amelia and Julia.
They happily settled into their routines, and life seemed good.

But their homecoming bliss didn’t last, as unsettling signs began to emerge.

Amelia and Julia both started to notice telltale signs that things weren't quite as they should be.

It started with a creepy feeling Amelia would get travelling home at night, like something was watching her from within the shadows.
Occasionally dark mist would drift across the roads, seeping from grids in the twilight of the late afternoon.
Strange low clouds increasingly dominated the skies, seeming to leach the very light from the sun.
Amelia noticed people looking drained of energy and Julia had also began noticing that people at school looked more fatigued and despondent.
Even Callum seemed distant at times, his eyes clouded by a darkness not his own.

That evening whilst eating dinner with her family, Amelia noticed her brother Cole staring vacantly past her.
"Cole!" Amelia said sharply, waving her hand in front of his face.
"Can you hear me? Are you okay?"
Cole continued staring straight ahead, his eyes glazed with a subtle flicker of orange deep within his pupils.
Amelia glanced worriedly at her parents.
"Mum, Dad, something's wrong with Cole!"

Her dad furrowed his brow.
"Son, snap out of it!" he said gruffly, snapping his fingers near Cole's ear.

After a couple of seconds, Cole suddenly blinked and shook his head as if coming out of a trance. "Huh? What?" he asked in confusion.
"You completely zoned out!" Amelia exclaimed.
"Your eyes were glowing orange and you weren't responding at all."

Cole scrunched his face up.
"Glowing eyes? What are you talking about? I'm fine, you weirdo."

Amelia looked anxiously at her parents. "Tell him!"
Amelia's mum gave her a sympathetic smile.
"You've had a long day sweetheart. I'm sure you thought you saw something."

Cole just shrugged and shovelled more food in his mouth. "Amelia's being crazy as usual," he mumbled through a mouthful.

That night in bed drifting off to sleep, Amelia felt a creeping influence, her skin turned to goosebumps and she shuddered, sitting bolt upright,
“I know that energy!” her palms were sweaty, she took a drink and reassured herself that she must have been dreaming. She settled herself once more and went to sleep.

A few days later during a storm Amelia's phone buzzed with a call from Julia. She quickly answered.
"Amelia,” Julia said, “Are you hearing this insane thunder?"
"Yes!" Amelia exclaimed. "In the rumbling, I can...it sounds like...that awful baleful laughter."
Amelia's throat tightened.
"I think he's here, Julia.
Weird things have been happening and now this...it can't be a coincidence if we’ve both heard it."

"What are we going to do?" Julia asked her voice wavering.
"Tomorrow after school let's meet at the tree.
We'll figure this out.” said Amelia, trying to sound braver than she felt.

The dismal truth now seemed undeniable, somehow, the Ashen King's evil essence had found a way to follow them back to Earth!

The following day, She and Julia met at the portal site, the old tree now lifeless and barren.
Amelia examined its ancient trunk, running her hands over its moss-covered bark.

She knew in her soul that if the Ashen king truly had made it through, then they had to prevent him from regaining his full, terrifying might.
But with her and Julias powers ineffective on Earth, Amelia realized they would need help.

Somehow, she had to find a way to reopen the mystical portal and return to the Realm of Reflections. Only by summoning their powerful allies there could they stand a chance of vanquishing the Ashen Kings evil once and for all.

Walking home feeling dejected, Amelia's head swirled with questions.
How had he survived? How had his evil managed to traverse the portal?
Why had her abilities vanished on Earth?
And most pressing, how could they hope to stop his encroaching darkness without magic or allies?

Arriving home, Amelia's mum, seeing her daughter's worried expression squeezed her shoulder gently.
"Everything okay? You seem a little burdened."

Amelia forced a smile.
"I'm fine, just...adjusting still."
She retreated to her room, mind racing.
There had to be an answer, some way to protect her family and hometown.
She just needed to have hope.

Staring out of her window into the gloom, Amelia knew she couldn't give up.
She had to keep trying to reopen that portal, no matter what it took.
The Ashen King may have begun darkening her world, but she would light it up again.

The following day Amelia and Julia met up and sat together, desperately trying to brainstorm ideas. After about an hour had passed, Julia suddenly jumped to her feet, grasping her amulet, her eyes widening.

"These amulets! Don't you remember what queen Visoo said about them linking us to their realm?" Julia exclaimed excitedly.

Hope surged within Amelia.
"You're right! Maybe they can help to reopen the portal!"

Joining hands, the girls focused intensely on their amulets, picturing the mountainous spires of Stormvale in their mind's eyes.
The gems flickered faintly, imbued with traces of the realm's magic.

Amelia and Julia poured all their energy into the artifacts, mentally projecting their urgent need to return.
The amulets shuddered, their light intensifying until finally a shimmering cosmic portal tore open before them!

CHAPTER 9

The Great Gathering

Life was bustling in Stormvale's great square when out of nowhere, a brilliant blaze of white light erupted in the air and remained several feet above the ground, causing an oval rip in the very essence of time.
Much to the delight of the Sky Folk, a slightly bewildered looking Amelia and Julia tumbled out and onto the ground!

A huge cheer went up from the gathered crowd.
Queen Visoo's voice rang out over the quickly hushing assembly.
"Welcome back, my beloved friends!"

She flew down majestically from her elevated balcony, flanked by her royal guards.
At the same moment, Prince Erevan skidded to a halt on his steed.

"Amelia, Julia!" the prince exclaimed, his eyes widening with surprise and delight.
"What are you doing here?"
He reached down and helped the girls to their feet.

Still regaining their balance, Amelia and Julia quickly explained how the Ashen King had somehow crossed over to Earth and was regaining power.
His creeping malevolence was already corrupting their hometown.

Queen Visoo's expression turned grave.
"This is troubling news. If left unchecked, the Ashen King threatens not just your world, but potentially all realms."

"Please, we need your help to stop him before it's too late," Amelia implored.

The queen nodded resolutely.
"Then we shall gather the Great Council at once.
All peoples of this realm must unite to address this threat; I shall inform the Guardians immediately."

Swiftly, royal messengers were dispatched across the lands, summoning representation from every clan and species.

Within days, huge numbers had gathered to the great crystal city of the Realms Guardians.
The grand crystal hall was filled to bursting with light beings, centaurs, satyrs, elves, sprites, pixies, dwarves, merfolk, shapeshifters, and more.
Speculation rippled through the packed crowd about this unprecedented gathering.

As Amelia and Julia entered the grand hall, the lively din of conversations echoed off the cavernous walls and towering multihued windows.
Representatives from every clan and species imaginable filled the room to bursting.
The girls felt overwhelmed trying to take it all in when suddenly a familiar melodic voice called out, "Amelia! Julia!"
They turned and saw Faven pushing gracefully through the crowd, her face alight with joy.
Unable to contain themselves, Amelia and Julia rushed forward throwing their arms around their dear friend.

"Oh Faven, it's so wonderful to see you again!"
Amelia implored, tears of happiness welling up in her eyes.
"Oh wow am I glad to see you," added Julia, squeezing Faven tightly.

"And I both of you, my brave sisters," Faven said, holding them close.
"When I heard the Great Gathering was being called, I simply had to come and stand by your side."

Finally releasing each other, the three friends sat amongst the throng, hands clasped together as they caught up and reminisced on all they had endured together.

Faven marvelled at how far Amelia and Julia had come, from their first disoriented steps into the magical realm, it already seemed like a lifetime ago.
"You both have grown so much, into such capable and compassionate souls," Faven praised, her voice brimming with pride.

"Whatever comes next, I know you shall rise to meet it."

Strengthened by her steadfast confidence and care, Amelia and Julia turned to face the crowded hall, comforted to have their dear companion supporting them once more.

The three guardians entered the hall, the glow of their radiance announcing their presence.
They raised their hands as one, and the lively hall fell silent.

Just before they began to speak and much to Amelia and Julias surprise, Ethaine the oracle appeared at their side, she nodded to them all respectfully then began whispering to Julia.

The guardians began,
"Esteemed friends and allies, we apologize for the abrupt summons, but a dire situation has arisen that endangers the balance between all realms."
They gestured toward Amelia and Julia.
"As many of you know, these brave humans aided us recently in banishing the Ashen King and his forces.
However, it seems that he persists and has somehow managed a crossing over to Earth to regain strength, threatening both their world and potentially our own.

This is a grave concern, as no resident of the Realms has ever been able to cross the portal outwardly and as far as we know, still can't!"
The crowd erupted into alarmed shouting and angry cries until Queen Visoo stood up and called for order.
"Please, friends! Right now, we must focus our efforts on finding a way to help Amelia and Julia put an end to the Ashen King's evil, before his chaos spreads."

With that, intense talks commenced on how best to empower and aid the girls in their quest.
Amelia felt humbled being at the centre of such a gathering of diverse leaders, all united by a common cause.
Ideas were passionately discussed at length as the daylight faded and night fell over the Realm.

Long into the night heated discussions continued until the first rays of dawn peeked over the crystal spires.
In the glaring rays of mornings first light, the leader of the Starbourne clan, Caelan, known for its brave and skilled scouts, stepped forward, clearing his throat delicately to address the crowd.
"If I may, I believe I know of magic that could help these brave souls in their fight."

Murmurs rippled through the throng at this proclamation.

"Many ages ago, one of our finest scouts found a hidden oasis situated far out in the desert expanses.
Our records say that it is home to an ancient tribe of sprites that according to the tales, granted a human wizard access to their lands and taught him powerful magic...magic he could wield even on Earth."

Shocked chatter broke out at this revelation. Caelan raised a hand for silence before continuing.

"This wizard mastered their teachings during his time at the Oasis. Perhaps they can pass on their gifts once more?"

At this, all eyes turned hopefully to Amelia and Julia.
Though nervous at the sudden responsibility, Amelia and Julia nodded dutifully.

Further discussions ensued until it was finally agreed that Julia would remain with Ethaine, joining the oracle on a pilgrimage of her own devising and though reluctant to separate, Julia took Amelia's hands and gave them a bolstering squeeze.
"You've got this! We'll see each other again soon. Just focus on mastering those spells," she said with an encouraging wink.
Heartened, Amelia turned to Caelan, thanking him for his suggestion.

Queen Visoo assigned her top scout, Daeryn of the Starbourne, to guide Amelia on the long and perilous route to the hidden Oasis.
Daeryn bowed graciously and stepped forward.

She was tall and slender, with a leggy, willowy figure that moved with athletic grace.
She had short, chestnut brown hair that framed her high cheekbones and a narrow chin, giving her an otherworldly, elfin look.
Her complexion was flawless, with just a smattering of freckles across her nose that only added to her charm.
She was wearing a form-fitting leather tunic and leggings that showed off her lithe physique.
Around her neck she wore her royal scout insignia on a silver chain, and she carried herself with an air of quiet confidence.
Though serious and stoic in demeanour, she had a genuinely warm smile that made Amelia feel special when it was directed at her for the first time and Daeryn's striking emerald green eyes looked deeply into Amelias approvingly.

At this moment, out of the corner of her eye Amelia noticed Prince Erevan eyeing her with thinly veiled admiration.
When he then volunteered to join their quest, Daeryn raised a skeptical eyebrow but remained silent.

After emotional farewells and some further preparations, the unlikely trio set off, to cross vast and varied landscapes on their journey to find the Oasis.

CHAPTER 10

Wizarding Waters

Flying low over grass plains the steeds' hooves barely brushing the land as they passed, playful jests and challenges were frequently exchanged between Prince Erevan and Daeryn as they vied for Amelia's attention. Though subtle, Amelia suspected deeper feelings at play in their competitive antics.

Prince Erevan and Daeryn possessed very different personalities but Amelia soon warmed to her new companions.

Daeryn was bold, witty and decisive, wasting no time in correcting what she saw as flawed thinking.

The prince was more philosophical and prone to musing, with an exaggerated sense of chivalry that made Amelia laugh.

As they journeyed on, Prince Erevan rode up alongside Amelia.

"This terrain ahead looks like it may be quite treacherous," he said gallantly. "Perhaps you would feel safer riding with me?"

Before Amelia could respond, Daeryn sidled up on her other side.

"Really?" she said satirically. "I'm sure Amelia is more than capable of handling herself."

Erevan flashed a coy smile.

"Of course, but it would be discourteous of me not to offer a prince's protection to a lady."

"How noble of you to protect her from the great dangers of flat grassy plains," Daeryn smirked.

The prince feigned offense.

"Mock my chivalry if you wish, but I shall not waiver."

Turning back to Amelia, he extended a hand. "Well, my lady?"

Suppressing a smile, Amelia politely declined.

"I appreciate the offer, but I'm quite alright riding on my own for now, thank you."

When they camped together at various stages of their journey, Amelia often found her gaze lingering on Daeryn's shapely silhouette backlit by the campfire.
There was an undeniable magnetism about her, she was mysterious yet approachable, standoffish yet kind-hearted beneath it all.
Amelia felt her cheeks flush whenever Daeryn's piecing green eyes would stare into her own, as if seeing into the depths of her soul and approving of what lay within.

Over time the terrain gradually shifted from the grass plains into river laced forests and eventually onwards to harsh, arid desert.
As they rode further into the desert something began to appear on the horizon, a strange shimmering came into view, distorting the skyline.
As they drew nearer, the seeming mirage coalesced into an oasis enclosed under a glittering opaque dome.

"Finally! The Waters of Light," said Daeryn, spurring her mount onwards with a quick tap of her heals.
To Amelias surprise Daeryn flew straight through the shimmering dome, followed quickly by the prince.
"Okay then," Amelia muttered under her breath, not wanting to appear hesitant and with a quick flick of her reins she entered into the domes mist, the delicately refreshing water vapour caressing her skin as she went.

"Oh... this place is beautiful." Amelia announced, as she emerged into the warmth of the rich and vibrant oasis, a colourful array meeting her eyes.
Exotic birds glided overhead amidst the canopy; their calls echoing back and forth.
She landed alongside the others, who stood surveying their new surroundings.

Amelia could feel the aura of ancient magic that hung over this paradise refuge and following a trail through the lush vegetation, they arrived at the pale sanded heart of the oasis where a clear pool of water glittered and shimmered, fed by sparkling fresh waterfalls that seemed to emanate from the canopy itself.

The pristine lagoon glowed as if charged by magical energy.
In the middle of the waters was a small island and hovering at its centre was what appeared to be a large glowing book, it was thick and bound by golden cords.

Amelia squinted at the tome but unease suddenly broke her focus and she felt her skin prickle as the foliage came alive with hushed whispering.
Small eyes peered out at them from within the vibrant flowery foliage.

Before they could react, Amelia, Daeryn and Eravan, found their wrists magically bound by glowing golden threads.
Dozens of small, winged sprites emerged wands drawn, their delicate features creased with suspicion and anger.
"Why have you trespassed here human?" demanded one guard, prodding Amelia with his tiny wand.

Thinking quickly, Amelia tried to explain the great gathering and their noble quest to vanquish the Ashen King.
But the sprites refused to believe that this strange trio could have any good intentions.

“What an unlikely group,” another sprite chimed, “Probably jealous of the wizards’ power I shouldn’t wonder.”
"Likely they mean to abuse the power of the tome!" accused another sentry.

Prince Erevan introduced himself with all the nobility he could muster and pleaded on their behalf, but the dismissive sprites floated the trio up into the air and moved them magically to an elevated mound of the central lagoon for judgement.

A crowned sprite moved to the fore.
Amelia desperately assured him that they wished no harm upon the magical oasis and indeed they had come here for the sprites help.

The king’s radiant aura flickered thoughtfully as he peered at the trio.
After several moments, he finally nodded,
"I sense you speak the truth human.
But consider this a warning... any attempts at the misuse of our beloved magic will bring dire consequences."

With a wave of his hand, their bonds vanished.
Relief swept over Amelia as she explained her plight in more detail.

“Why don’t you ask the human Wizard for help then?” he said after listening carefully to Amelias story.

Amelia's mind reeled.
A human wizard who had learned magic from these sprites. And he was apparently still alive after all these centuries?

“We taught him some wonderful magical spells and he became quite adept under our tutorage.
Our magic is the oldest there is.” He continued.
“It doesn’t just manifest and flow about willy-nilly, it has to be mastered, crafted, these spells must be cast, and the power and purity of their effect lies in the innate nature of the caster.”

“This is true magic”, beamed the Sprite King, his chest puffing a little with pride.
“Its power is contained within the wielder themselves, and it resides wherever they do!

All the magical incantations one could ever want for, are contained within that Tome there.”
He pointed his wand toward the bound floating tome they had spotted upon first entering the oasis.

Amelia thought for a moment,
"Please, where can we find this wizard?" Amelia implored the Sprite King.
"If he mastered your teachings, perhaps he can help us defeat the Ashen King once and for all?
I had intended to ask for your aid in teaching me your grace, so that I might face down the Ashen Kings evil back in my home world, but this may be an even better solution, don’t you think?”

The winged monarch considered this carefully.

"Hmm... yes, Abe was his first name, though he had a middle name, Merlinius as I recall, you know I've quite forgotten his last name. A stubborn yet dedicated man he was, I grew quite fond of him.
The last we saw of him was when he'd finally mastered his training and returned to your world, consumed with defending it from some great evil.
I cannot say for certain where he dwells now after all this time. But our records indicate we sent him back through a portal in the northern mountains."

Thanking the king profusely, Amelia, Daeryn and Prince Erevan swiftly departed the oasis.

They flew at speed across the desert, then over some unfamiliar rocky terrain until the northern peaks came into view and anticipation gripped them.
Would this mythical wizard still be alive?
And if so, would he deem their cause worthy? Surely, he must.

Navigating some treacherous ravines and a jagged winding pass, they combed the mountains for any sign of the portal.
Just as despair began setting in, Daeryn's sharp eyes spotted an unusual formation of rock spires.
"That must be it!" she exclaimed.

Setting their steeds down, the trio hesitantly approached the magical looking gateway.
Ancient runes surrounded the arch, but it all looked long dormant.

"So how do we activate it?" Prince Erevan mused, reaching out to touch the mystical archway.

"Oouuuuphhh!!!" The sharp sound of air being sucked between pursed lips made the prince jump back startled.
"You don't want to go touching that, you being both nobility and of the Realm."
Said the Oracle Ethaine, who'd seemingly appeared out of thin air, accompanied by Julia.

"Julia!" gasped Amelia as she lunged forward, embracing her with a big hug.

“Now, mind what I’ve told you Julia.” Continued Ethaine, fixing Julia with a steely look.

Julia nodded then smiled at the group before stepping toward the stone archway.

As she did, the runes instantly blazed to life, a vortex appeared in the archway, churning with ever increasing speed.
Shielding her eyes from the intense light, Julia stepped through.
She felt the now familiar falling sensation before her feet thudded down on solid ground.

As her vision adjusted, she saw that she was standing before the mouth of an intricate cave system.

"Well, I hope this is the right place," she thought, peering warily into the rocky tunnels.
Moving cautiously, she entered the caverns.
Glowing crystals illuminated the walls, reflecting off subterranean pools.

It reminded Julia of the Caverns of Whispers. She hoped this one held less danger.
As she ventured inward, she paused. Straining her ears, she could detect faint notes echoing through the caves, like a lyre being plucked.

Guided by the music, she continued ahead until the tunnel opened up.

A gentle waterfall trickled over smooth rock polished by time, and flowed into a shimmering pool below.
seated comfortably beside it, dipping his toes in, eyes closed whilst his fingers strummed the curious instrument, was an old bearded man in long robes.

"Greetings young traveller," his gravelly voice called out.
"It has been an age since anyone entered this sacred place."
Finally opening his eyes, he studied Julia with an intense, penetrating gaze.

Swallowing down nerves, she stepped forward.
"I have come seeking the wizard Abe. Is that you?" Julia asked tentatively.

The old man raised one bushy eyebrow.
"Indeed I am, though few now recall that name, mmmh or any of the others for that matter," the wizard mumbled under his breath.
"Even fewer would recognize this face nowadays." He chuckled, stroking his long grey beard pensively.

"But the better question is, why do you, young stranger, seek me out?"

Relieved beyond measure, Julia introduced herself and quickly delved into the urgent need of his help against the spreading darkness of the Ashen King. She left no detail unexplained, her passion and desperation evident with each word.

Abe listened silently, other than the sound of his feet swishing the cool water, his expression unreadable.
After she had finished her plea, he closed his eyes again, as if meditating deeply on all he had heard.

When finally he spoke, his gravelly voice was tinged with sorrow.
"This Ashen King you describe, his malevolence is familiar to me.
Long ago I faced a similar evil. I had hoped my efforts would safeguard both realms eternally."

He sighed heavily, as if the weight of ages was upon him.
"But it seems darkness always finds a way back."

Opening his eyes wider, resolve shone through the fatigue and sadness.
"I shall help you as I am able. But know young Julia that the magic for such an undertaking is no small feat, it requires risk! maybe even sacrifice."
Julia nodded but could hardly contain her curiosity and so after much coaxing, the wizard finally agreed to share his tale of battling the ancient evil long ago.

The elderly wizard conjured a fire that crackled softly as he sank down with a weary sigh.
Placing his instrument carefully and removing his hat, his grey hair wisped around his wrinkled forehead.
He suddenly looked every bit of his unfathomable age.

"In my youth," he began, "I was much like you... hungry for adventure, for purpose.
I stumbled upon a portal to the realms by chance and felt destiny's pull to enter."

Julia listened, enraptured, as Abe wove a story of discovering mentors, confronting spectres, and ultimately overcoming a dark force by believing in his own light and using Sprite magic he had so eagerly learned.

But this Ashen King seemed even more dangerous, thought Julia.

Noticing her furrowed brow, Abe held up a finger.
"Take heart, young one. You still have much to discover."

Crossing the cave, he stood, waving his hand over a dark section of wall. At once, a hidden doorway opened in the rockface, revealing a secret chamber.

"We shall find the means for victory in here!" He smiled at Julia's awed expression. "Come."

Julia followed eagerly and upon entering the room Abe conjured a light which gradually grew brighter revealing a circular room, containing at its centre, a solitary stone pillar, upon which sat two very ornate rings.
One was golden and inlayed with symbols; Abe picked it up.
"This is The Ring of Dispel, given to me by a very special lady who resided at a beautiful lake, many years ago. Its power can dispel any enchantment."
"Here," said Abe handing it to Julia.
"Wow its heavy." Remarked Juila as she eyed it closely, rolling it about in her cupped hands.

"And this...this is the mighty Seal of Draconem." said Abe as he handed a large silver ring of mirror finish, inlaid with tiny fragments of black, to Julia.
"This one was entrusted to me by a wise and ancient dragonkin, it's imbued with tiny fragments from one of his claws."
"Its power can imprison any kind of Demon."

The final confrontation was coming.

And Julias faith was now becoming stronger, that maybe this time, with their combined efforts, they might just succeed.

CHAPTER 11

Rivalry Rekindled

Back in the northern peaks, Prince Erevan, Daeryn and Amelia glanced from one to another then back at the now dormant archway.
"Best get yourselves back to the oasis, get some of that magical learning done Amelia." said Ethaine sternly.
Amelia looked first at prince Erevan who was stood with his mouth partially open as if looking for the right words, then to Daeryn who rolled her eyes and mounted up in one graceful motion.
Amelia turned back to Ethaine... but the oracle was gone.

After a rather moody and noticeably silent ride together the trio arrived once again at the oasis.

Days went by swiftly soon turning into weeks as Amelia immersed herself, under the guidance of the Sprite King, into learning various magical spells contained within the ancient floating tome.

She perfected intricate incantations, summoning lightning, conjuring protective shields, and even manipulating the elements.

Though these abilities could be used back on Earth, Amelia clung to the hope that the mysterious wizard would be found and Julia would soon be back with her again.

As her skills grew, so too did her homesickness.
She missed her family, her own bed, the simple comforts of home.
She was missing Julia and Faven too.

Though Daeryn and Prince Erevan's playful rivalry persistently distracted her, in quiet moments her mind wandered.
Had the Ashen King's darkness taken root now back on Earth?

One evening while practicing spells, Daeryn approached her, concern in her piercing green eyes.
"Your thoughts drift away from us," she said.
Amelia blushed, caught off guard by the scout's perceptiveness.
"Forgive me. I just..." Her words trailed off helplessly.

Daeryn lifted Amelia's chin, meeting her gaze.
"You need not explain. I see the longing in your eyes. Home calls to your spirit."

Amelia found herself lost for a moment in Daeryn's understanding smile.
The scout's hand lingered a second too long upon her cheek.
Across the oasis Prince Erevan watched the intimate exchange, his nostrils flaring jealousy at their closeness.
Posturing proudly, he strode over.
"Pardon my intrusion but I wish to discuss our future plans." His tone was clipped and formal.

Daeryn arched one eyebrow coolly.
"Your highness." She replied, courteously bowing, though ever so slightly.

As Erevan launched into an unnecessary reiteration of their plans for when Amelia had mastery of the requisite spells, his pompous demeanour made her stifle a laugh.

Later, alone under the stars, her thoughts turned to her dear friend.
Where was Julia now?
What wisdom was she gaining from her time with the Oracle that could aid their quest?

Amelia's heart swelled with love for her home, for Julia's company, for adventure itself.
She hugged her knees, comforted by the blanket of constellations overhead, reminding her of the night skys back home.
There was still much to accomplish here. But soon, she would return home.
She had to trust that.

After weeks turned into months Amelia's confidence in spell casting escalated rapidly under the exquisite guidance of the sprites until one

morning, she inexplicably felt that she was ready, and should return to Earth to once again face down the Ashen King.
The sprites agreed that she was well versed now with a powerful repertoire of spells.

“Remember Amelia the power and purity of these spells comes from within you, from your intent.”
The sprite kings last words echoed in her mind as she, Daeryn and prince Erevan arrived at a new portal not far from the oasis, exactly where the sprites had directed them.

Daeryn and Erevan embraced Amelia making her vow to return as soon as she could, then without hesitation Amelia stepped into the swirling array.

A kaleidoscope of colours emersed her senses until suddenly with a soft thud Amelia was back in the woodland near her new academy.

She quickly glanced around, fully expecting to find her hometown corrupted and oppressed under the veil of darkness.
But shockingly, everything appeared normal.

The skies were blue, people smiled and laughed as she left the woods and walked on towards town. There was no sign of the Ashen King's evil influence.

"How can this be?" Amelia wondered aloud.
"The darkness should have spread unchecked in our absence."

Suddenly her phone buzzed in her pocket, “Oh my phone” Amelia took it out surprised to see a message from Julia.
“Meet us at the swings!”
“Us?” thought Amelia, when did Julia get back, and who is she with!?”

Amelia hurried toward the park and upon arriving she spotted Julia stood with an elderly looking character, who could only be a wizard! she thought, feeling a sudden rush of excitement.

“Amelia!” Shouted Julia, rushing over to embrace her. “This is Abe!”

Abe stroked his beard thoughtfully.
"Amelia, my pleasure, I've heard much about you, all good of course." he added with a smile.

Amelia and Julia both interrupted one another simultaneously, each having so many questions they wanted to ask of the other, they laughed.
"You first," said Julia.

"I don't think we have time for that just now," interrupted Abe.
"Everything seems a little too right," Abe continued, closing his eyes.
"I sense a subtle wrongness threading through the harmony around us, dark magic leaves traces.
Let us examine the fabric of this reality more closely.

Julia, the golden ring if you please."

Julia reached into her zipper pocket,
"Here Abe, open your eyes!" said Juila with a sense of urgency as she tossed the ring to Abe, who caught it deftly, his eyes still shut, and slid it firmly onto his finger.

Abe's eyes shot open.
"Oh dear! A powerful illusion enchantment has been cast! The Ashen King hides his corruption behind a false veil of normality."

"Can you break the enchantment?" asked Julia, panic growing in her voice.

"No, only the caster can dismantle such magic. However now that I see through the illusion, we can trace it to its source."

Like a compass, Abe's outstretched palm was drawn toward the spell's origin.
"Come, quickly now!"

The girls hurriedly followed Abe as he set off at a pace.
Eventually they arrived at an inconspicuous warehouse on the outskirts of the city.

"The Ashen King lurks inside," Abe intoned confidently.
"Be prepared for anything."

Amelias heart began to pound as they cautiously approached, ready to counter whatever vile forces awaited.
But as they stepped inside, no horrors lay in ambush, only a young, unassuming boy.

He looked up, and Amelia gasped.
"Cole? What are you doing here?"

Her little brother gave a malicious grin, his eyes flashing fiery orange.
"Welcome sister. My master has been expecting you."
The shock of the Ashen King's possession paralyzed Amelia and her heart sank, seeing her beloved little brother possessed by the Ashen King's malevolence.

"Fight him, Cole!" she implored. "Don't let him control you!"

Cole's face changed into a sneer.
"Your brother cannot hear you. His soul is bound to my will!" The Ashen King taunted through him.

Amelia felt hot tears spill down her cheeks.
She had to save her brother. But how could she combat this evil without harming him?

Cole's face twisted cruelly. "Foolish girl, your brother is gone. Now you will join him!"

The Ashen King raised Cole's arms, summoning a raging firestorm toward Amelia.

Responding on pure instinct from her magical training, she thrust out her palms, meeting the flames with an icy torrent of her own.
The two elemental forces collided in a sizzling stalemate.

Abe's voice rang out firmly.
"The possession can be broken! Focus your magic on expelling the darkness from your brother."

Closing Quickly Abe erected a shimmering orbital shield around them.

Amelia tapped into the magical current within her spirit. She felt the light of her love for Cole burning intensely.
Channelling it through her hands, she released a powerful flurry of spells, sending intensely bright shapes of several luminescent colours hurtling through the warehouse and enveloping Cole, making him cry out.
He writhed, the Ashen King's dark essence fighting back viciously.

"Don't give up!" urged Amelia.
"Cole, I know you're in there! You have to fight!" she yelled.

Her magic slammed into Cole, making him scream as violent spasms wracked his body.
For a moment, his familiar eyes locked onto Amelia's. "Don't...give...up on...me," he gasped before the Ashen King regained control.

"We have to strike together!" Abe shouted over the magical maelstrom.

Empowered by Cole's plea, Amelia unleashed every ounce of magic left in her spirit.
Abe raised his arms and closing his eyes he unleashed huge plumes of vibrant magic which streamed from his fingertips, intertwining the Amelia's magic.
The mystical energy built to a thundering crescendo, shaking the very ground beneath their feet.

With a blood-curdling howl, the dark entity was wrenched from Cole's body in an explosive vortex of light and shadow.
The spectral Ashen King coalesced overhead, writhing in fury, red eyes blazing.
His smoky claws stretched forth, raking the air leaving smouldering scars.

"Impossible! I cannot be defeated again!" the shadow roared.

But Amelia stood fast, her hands aglow with purifying light, ready to meet the ancient evil with all her courage.

"You underestimate the strength of family. Their love makes them more powerful than you will ever be," Abe responded resolutely.

“Now Julia!” implored Abe.
“The Seal of Draconem, wear it!”

“Me!” exclaimed Julia.
“PUT IT ON!!!” Boomed Abe.

Julia thrust into her pocket sliding the oversized ring onto her finger. Immediately the ring shrank clasping her skin firmly.

Julia trembled as an immense surge of power rushed through her entire being, she felt... invincible! Her hands instinctively shot up to her eye level, palm over palm, as torrents of brilliant white light leapt from the ring.

The Ashen King screamed as the beams of light cascaded around him, snaring him from all directions.

His smoky form was dragged through the air against his will, as the power of the seal overwhelmed the demon, reducing him to wisps of inky blackness and finally sucking him into the ring, until with a final enraged scream, nothing!... only echoing silence remained.

Dabbing beads of sweat from his matted forehead Abe leaned forward, “Hmm, I best take that,” he said, sliding the ring from a shocked looking Julia’s still trembling finger.
Abe placed his hands on Julias shoulders, “Well done!” he smiled.

Gasping with relief, Amelia cradled Cole, his eyes now clear.
"You did it," he whispered. "You saved me."

Abe and Julia laid comforting hands onto Amelia and Coles shoulders as the group huddled together and began to chuckle in relief, forever bound by their triumph over the Ashen King.

Abe sighed heavily then spoke, “My dear Amelia, Julia and Cole... always have hope, believe in courage, and love deeply, for light ever prevails over darkness.”

CHAPTER 12

Symphony of Unity

In the days after their victory over the Ashen King, Amelia found her thoughts continuously drifting back to the Realm of Reflections.
She knew how important it was to inform the leaders of the Realm that their great help had been a success and that both worlds were now safe.
In truth she also missed her friends there deeply, especially Faven, Daeryn, and Prince Erevan.

Without question she was much happier at school now and life was good, but she yearned for the sense of wonder and belonging that she felt in the Realms mystical lands.

That evening whilst gazing at her amulet, an idea came to her.
She picked up her phone,
"Julia, do you think we could reopen the portal and visit the realm one last time?"

At the other end of the phone, Julia's eyes lit up.
"I was hoping you'd suggest that! I'd love to let everyone know we succeeded."

That weekend they returned to the tree and Joining hands, they focused intensely on their amulets like before.
This time, the portal opened almost instantly in a dazzling flash of light.

Steadying their nerves, they stepped through, a kaleidoscope of colours swirling around them.
With a sudden rush of magic, their feet touched down on the luminescent purple grass of that familiar mystical meadow of their very first arrival. They were back!

"Welcome!" cried Faven, rushing forward to embrace them.

"We sensed the portal opening and I just knew it must be you!"

Amelia and Julia hugged her joyfully.
"We did it, Faven! The Ashen King is imprisoned in a ring back on Earth. Abe has it secured."

Faven's radiance glowed brighter.
"Wonderful news! Come, we must go to the city and inform the guardians right away."

Amelia's heart swelled. Being back felt so right. Like she had returned to a part of herself.

They entered the beauty of the crystal city and were quickly met by Balan, Torin and Valdis, whose auras glowed brightly.
The three guardians wasted no time in congratulating Amelia and Julia, joy evident in their voices.

“Your heroic efforts will forever remain a part of our history, the courage, kindness and the incredible collaborations you’ve forged here will never be forgotten.”
The guardians bowed graciously.
“We will commune with Queen Visoo, she will be eager to hear of this great news.”

Faven guided the girls to a plush area where they sat together discussing all that had happened back on Earth.
Amelia, Julia and Faven were deep in conversation when a commotion outside signalled that an envoy of Stormvale riders had arrived to collect them.

Before long, the group were touching down in the city square, swarmed by delighted sky folk.
Prince Erevan pushed through the crowd, sweeping Amelia into a tight hug.

"You brilliant, brave girl! We knew you would prevail!" pride shining in his eyes.

Daeryn expertly slunk alongside and squeezed her hand warmly, the depth of caring unspoken yet understood between them.
Amelia felt her cheeks blush under the attention.

Soon, trumpets rang out as Queen Visoo emerged onto her balcony.
"Rejoice! The Ashen King is no more a threat!" she declared to resounding cheering and hollering.

At the queens insistence, Amelia and Julia recounted the final battle, the crowd listened in awed silence.
When they described Cole's possession and salvation, many wept.

"Your selflessness and love saved both realms," said Queen Visoo, her voice thick with emotion.
"You will always have a place here and a special place in my heart."

Later, alone with Daeryn and the prince, the three friends walked together reminiscing.
Amelia wished the reunion could last forever but no sooner had she entertained the thought than it was interrupted by the oracle Ethaine, making yet another of her rare public appearances!

She beckoned to Amelia and then to Julia, who was becoming flustered by the amorous attention of one of the queens' elite guards.

Once closer, Ethaine encompassed them in a glowing aura, transporting them to her grotto.

Inside her cozy candle lit cave, Ethaine pulled some strange looking goggles over her head, they were copper coloured, their shape resembling an Owls head, with thick emerald lenses.
The oracle gazed into the distance intently.
"My, my... I see wonderous things in your futures."

She smiled, placing a hand on each of their cheeks.
"Trust in yourselves. Your lives have just begun.
Permit an old woman to share a story with you before we return to Stormvale."

The oracle fixed them with a knowing look and a twinkle in her eye as she began.

"... A traveller journeys through a dim, foggy forest, unsure of the path ahead.
With each step, shadows dance and play tricks on the eyes.
Strange sounds echo between the trees.
The way forward is unclear.

As the traveller continues, the fog grows denser, enveloping them in a cool, grey veil.
The forest floor turns damp and mossy underfoot.
Still the traveller persists, compelled by an unseen force.

Further and further into the haze they walk, losing track of time and distance.
The sounds of the forest fade away, leaving only the padding of footsteps over soft earth.

The air turns heavy, laden with the scent of loam and leaves.
The traveller's breath slows, matching the languid pace of their strides.
Their mind empties, thoughts fading into the fog.

The trees themselves seem to whisper and beckon, leaning in close as if to share long held secrets.
But their voices are too muted to understand.

Time stretches on as the traveller drifts through this strange, muted world.
The path winds on aimlessly, destination unknown.

Eventually, the traveller emerges from the mist.
They stand at the edge of the forest, gazing out into an open, sunlit meadow.
The fog lingers at their back, the forest now a distant memory.
With clearing eyes, the traveller steps forward into the light. The journey continues..."

The Oracle shook the girls' shoulders and laughed. "Time for Stormvale."

The next two days were filled with celebrations as all the realm's peoples gathered to Stormvale, conversing merrily and savouring exquisite foods.

The grand banquet hall was alive with music and laughter as the winged sky folk erupted in jubilant revelry, their uplifting songs echoing between the spires.

Centaurs laughed heartily, their hooves clip-clopping on the polished stone floor in time to the music as they toasted the young heroines with goblets of honey mead.
Elven bards added to the lively melody with their ornate instruments.
Even merfolk appeared frolicking in the moonlit pools of the mountain, their iridescent tails sending sprays of water sparkling through the air.

Whilst the feasting, singing and dancing continued, Queen Visoo and her guards led Amelia and Julia to a high tower balcony, both girls wondering what was happening.
"For you, brave souls!" declared the Queen.

Amelia and Julia heard the awed cries of the crowd below as the sky suddenly exploded with dazzling fireworks.
The first soared like a comet, leaving a huge trail of golden sparks in its wake.

Then came a cascade of indigo stars, like a giant waterfall frozen in time that hung in the air, drifting as it slowly faded from sight.

The crowd below gasped in unison as an enormous silver serpent shimmered across the sky and spiralled gracefully upwards, growing smaller until it vanished into the vastness of the night.

Immediately after, the sky lit up with countless glittering flowers carpeting the blackness before exploding into fluttering butterflies that then gently dissolved on the breeze.

The night had become a canvas, and the fireworks its paint.
Amelia put her arm around Julia, both their faces glowing with happiness.

As the wonderous night gradually rolled into morning, it was finally time to depart.
After many fond farewells and tearful hugs, Daeryn pressed a glittering crystal leaf into Amelia's hand.

"So you don't forget me."

Prince Erevan kissed her hand gallantly, his usual bravado replaced by sincerity.

Faven hugged them tightly. "We will see one another again. Our hearts are as one."

With a multitude of mixed feelings, Amelia and Julia stepped through the portals radiance.

When they emerged back on Earth, Amelia turned the crystal leaf over in her palm, its facets throwing rainbows of light.

"Do you think we will go back someday?" she asked Julia wistfully.
Julia squeezed her hand.
"I hope so. But for now, let's focus on living our lives to the fullest right here."

Amelia nodded, blinking back happy tears.
Their great journey was over but the realm would live forever in their hearts.

And though they walked in a different world now, she and Julia in many ways would always remain citizens of that magical realm hidden across the stars.

The End

...for now...

Printed in Great Britain
by Amazon

36220529R00061